The Silver Lining

Hollie Furniss

Published by Hollie Furniss, 2023.

THE SILVER LINING

First edition. April 6, 2023.

Copyright © 2023 Hollie Furniss.

ISBN: 979-8201792251

Written by Hollie Furniss.

Prologue
Zoe

Autumn came, and my heart broke.

Sucking in the last mouthful of brisk air, I stepped through the automated doors and along the glossy, long corridors that felt like my second home. Unlike a hospital, the place attempted to masquerade as something else. Bright, lime green splashes of colour dotted around the space, trying to make things less depressing. It didn't work. The smell of antiseptic permeated every room, silently and invisibly revealing its true purpose.

I was making my daily visit to the hospice where my mother was slowly deteriorating from cancer. Ten years prior, she'd managed to beat the damn thing, now it had come back more ferocious than ever.

Desensitised, I sailed through the maze of doors on autopilot, my doc-martin boots squeaking embarrassingly with each stride, but my focus remained firm.

As I approached my mother's ward, I could tell something was different. The nurses didn't greet me with a smile and courteous "Hello," as usual. Their faces were solemn with hooded eyes and knitted brows - picture postcard concern.

I rushed over to my mother's bed to see the trigger. My mother, my beautiful, radiant, and lovely mother was a shell of herself. All the glowing life was gone. Left was this tiny, sunken, grey person with closed eyes and rasping breaths.

The nurses confirmed my darkest fear. It was time. All I could do was sit by her side, and hold what was left of her fragile hand as a nurse called my father.

It was no good. She passed before he arrived. I was glad really. It felt right, just us two. I was birthed into this world by this great woman, and she left this world by my side.

When my father arrived, grief seized his former face and frame into a pained stranger; the cancer had somehow shrunken him too. His skin seemed ashen, and his eyes were as lifeless as hers. His hair bounced loosely with flecks of silver, no longer bound in place with pomade, as he sobbed against her hardened chest.

When he eventually peeled himself off her limp body and silenced his heaving cries, we embraced one another as grieving family members do. At that time, I didn't know what my father was, but I was about to find out.

1

Zoe

St. Leonard's Hospice was a twenty-minute drive from Haxby. I travelled along the A64 in a haze towards the house I grew up in. Beyond my beaten-up Vauxhall Astra spanned stretches of sprawling road. The engine revved as I pushed on the acceleration and snaked through cars. In the background, the radio crackled indistinct lyrics. The volume was too low to make out which song was playing.

Halted at a set of traffic lights, I caught sight of my reflection in the rear-view mirror. Blotches of crimson peppered my skin, and mascara smeared around my swollen eyes. Horns beeped, signalling the green light. I just had time to wipe some of the blackness away with the end of my woollen jumper before I reached my destination.

As I approached the drive, I could see my father's inky Ford. He'd made it back before me; lights illuminated the downstairs signifying life.

Stepping inside felt like an imposition, even though it had once been my home too. Without my mum's presence, the rooms felt colder, smaller - all too quiet. Her laughter could no longer be heard echoing through the hallways. Her silhouette no longer hastily flurrying around cleaning and tidying. Isn't it strange how you only recall the good times when thinking back on a deceased loved one?

My eyes caught a glimpse of her favourite mug on the kitchen side. I'd bought it for her as a birthday present one year. It was adorned with metallic, gold feathers against a soft pink background, although some of the metallics had worn off. On the front were the words, 'Mothers don't sleep, they just worry with their eyes closed.' I remember after she had opened it she said, "You know me so well, Zoe!"

I had. She was always a worrier. Ever since I was born, my mother, Grace, would be fretting over my every move. Learning how to swim, she was petrified that I'd drown. She never let me swim without her eyes burning into the back of my neck. All the other mothers would be nattering away to friends or buried deep into a book. Not my mum. She convinced herself that if she couldn't see me, something bad would happen. Learning how to ride a bike was a nightmare.

"What if you fall off?" she'd say.

"Then I will just get back on," I'd respond.

Once I had conquered the wheels and proven myself capable, she still wasn't satisfied. "Don't go too fast or too far. Stay where I can see you."

My innate clumsiness hadn't helped. I still have scars scattered across my kneecaps. Even as a teenager, I had to be in eyesight.

"It isn't you I don't trust," she'd say.

Her oppression wore on our relationship for a period because I let it, and the guilt of that swept through me – drowned me. Her precious, motherly concern was gone, and I longed for it – ached for it.

All those memories flooded my mind as I crept through her house, like an intruder. It was so strange seeing photographs hung on the walls of her smiling. I'd seen those photographs a million times, and I'd never looked at them the way I did then, frozen in time, alive, happy, healthy.

With the biggest smile, always adorned in red lipstick, surrounded by curled, blonde locks. I turned myself away and began sorting through her things.

One of the jobs I knew I'd have to do sooner or later was sorting through her clothes. There were items I wanted to keep for myself: an oversized jacket she'd loved in the '80s and said she would give me one day, and of course her wedding dress – a puffy, lace meringue that was truly horrendous but somehow looked sensational in her wedding pictures.

Up to this point, my father, James, and I had floated about in our separate grieving bubbles. We'd never been tactile. All my life, my father had been on the fringes of my existence, tight-lipped but present, involved just enough to know me as a daughter but not enough to know me as a person. Death only magnified our awkwardness.

As I made my way up the stairs, my father intercepted me.

"Where are you going?" Despite having lived in Haxby for decades, an Irish accent still lingered on his tongue. The same accent that seduced my mother all those years ago.

I stopped my ascent, not looking him in the eye. "I want some of mum's things."

I could practically feel his forehead crinkling. "What things?" he questioned abruptly.

"Just some clothes, if that's okay?"

When he didn't badger me further, I pressed on, taking it as a sign of agreeance.

I continued up the stairs and headed to my mum's bedroom. Browsing through her cluttered wardrobe, I feared I wouldn't be able to find her infamous jacket, but right at the back, practically the last item (as it always is), was the shoulder-padded piece I was searching for. I immediately smiled as I pulled it out into the light. It smelt a little fusty, but it looked as gorgeous as I remembered. It had large lapels and sturdy gold buttons dotted down the front with marvellous puffed sleeves. I slipped it on, hugging it around me.

Then I began to weep.

I buckled over and let the sadness wash over me. I knew this day had been coming, but the realisation that my mother would never return hit me like a bulldozer. It was at that moment, I felt something scratch against my skin. I thought it was a label in the lining of the jacket, but when I took it off, I saw a hidden pocket inside and a piece of paper poking out. I stared at it for a few seconds, wondering what it could be before gently taking it out and unfolding it. The letter was addressed to me.

2

Zoe

*D*ear darling Zoe,

I suppose you have found this letter in the wake of my death. It feels strange to be writing this knowing I will not be around at the moment you are reading these words.

You are the most wonderful daughter a mother could ask for. I feel so lucky to have made such a perfect person. You were the ray of sunshine in my life. The one thing that kept me going during my darkest of days.

I can't believe I won't be around to watch you grow up. To meet your future husband or hold my future grandchildren. No matter how sad you feel now, know this feeling will not last forever. Let it pass quickly, so you may get on with living your life! I will never forget you, and I will always love you. I hope after I tell you what I am about to say, you will still love me too.

I am so sorry. I have been keeping a secret from you. I hope you are alone before you read on.

Your father is a bad man. A man you need to stay away from. I have reason to think he is responsible for many killings. I know this will come as a shock, but I need you to be wary. I did not have the strength to confront your father, and I am begging you to not confront him either. He is capable of horrendous acts. This I know first-hand. As my dying wish, please obey this instruction. Rid yourself of him and start a new life.

I love you so much,

Mum x

The letter trembled in my hands. My father was a bad man, a killer? *Why had my mother never spoken of this before?*

Suddenly, I heard footsteps creaking up the staircase, and I knew I needed to leave. I stuffed the letter into my pocket and fled past my father, calling to him as I hurried, "I have to leave, I forgot I need to be somewhere, sorry!" I didn't stay to hear his reply.

The front door slammed on my way out. I frantically opened my car door and ignited the engine. I paused momentarily to glance back at the upstairs window. The figure of my dad stood, watching. After wiping my wet eyes, I pushed the car into first gear and drove off.

All the way home, my ears filled with the drumming of my heart. My limbs were but mere mechanics as my mind was hijacked by my emotions. I felt elsewhere, otherworldly.

Somehow, I made it back unscathed and parked up. The sky outside was transitioning to dusk, awash with burnt orange and cobalt. My hands still gripped the steering wheel as all the heat from the car evaporated. I don't know how long I sat there like that - not knowing how to use my limbs or mind for action. Eventually, I pushed the car door open and ambled to my property, forcing my feet forward.

Inside the salvation of my own home, I flicked on the hallway light, and it buzzed yellow. I sank into a heap on the floor and uncrumpled the letter once more. I could feel my heart quickening and breath racing.

What was going on?

How could my mother believe her husband was a murderer? How could my mother believe my *father* was a murderer? The same man who taught me how to speak French and how to play the guitar (albeit badly). The same man who defended me against bullies and told me everything was going to be alright when I didn't make my grades. My head swam with confusion. Nothing made sense. It was only then that I realised I'd left the jacket in my haste, sprawled out on my mum's bed like a deflated ghost. I wondered what he thought when he saw it.

That night, I went to bed with sore eyes that were empty of tears. I tossed and turned for hours, replaying my mother's final words, final warnings. Eventually, I drifted off. Even then, my mind wouldn't let me rest. Images flashed constantly before my closed eyelids. I dreamt of my childhood. I could see my parents laughing and canoodling at Christmas while they prepared dinner. I was smiling at them through a slight gap into the kitchen as I played with my new toys. Festive music sang dimly in the background, and I could feel the warmth of the house.

My dream skipped to the evening. The house felt chillier, the table cleared of food. My mother was slurring her words, saying things I didn't understand. Without warning, my father grabbed her by the throat. So hard her drink spilt down the sofa, and her eyes grew desperately red and wet. Her hands frantically pulled at his fingers. No words could escape her lips. Her breath faulted and her gaze glossed over as if she was about to lose consciousness, but then footsteps interrupted them.

His hands leapt from her throat. Face empty, he hurried to straighten her appearance before sitting her back down. My mum began wiping the sofa down as the living room door gently swung open. *I* tiptoed in, sheepish and tired. I curled up on the sofa and started watching the TV, acting completely oblivious to the scene prior.

My body woke in revolt. Was that a memory or a nightmare? I could never remember my father laying a finger on my mother. Could I? They had a great marriage.

In the light of the morning, I had an urge to retrace my past. No better place to start than photo albums. I scattered my family's life across my wooden floor. From baby pictures to holiday snaps, it was all there. We looked like a normal family, didn't we? I needed a second opinion.

Despite the early start, my best friend Vivienne came to me within twenty minutes of my phone call. "I'm looking through photographs of my mother. It feels bloody depressing all on my lonesome. Join me?" I pleaded. I'd already texted her about my mum's death the day before. She knew how much I needed her.

"I'll be there with your favourite Starbucks in less than half-an-hour."

Viv was the very definition of loyal and true. If anyone could help me, it was her.

3

Zoe

Viv rushed through my front door without knocking. In her manicured hands were two cups of cappuccino. A kiss imprint of cherry signalled which one was hers. Even in her haste, she'd had time to apply a layer of crimson to her lips.

"Come here you," Viv said as she placed the cups down on my scratched, second-hand coffee table and hugged me so tight that I got a mouth full of her fiery red tresses. I could feel the silk of her scarf too – one from her collection of annual presents from me.

"Thank you for coming," I whispered over her shoulder, feeling her slender silhouette between my arms. She smelled comforting, familiar. I reluctantly relinquished my embrace and stepped back with intent.

Viv took my hands into hers, reaffirming our connection. She always was the more tactile one between us.

"How are you holding up?" she asked, her jade eyes fixed to mine.

How was I feeling? I settled on, "Confused. Sad. Angry."

As if sensing my upset, Barney, my cat, weaved through my legs purring.

"You are going to feel all those things," she said as we gravitated towards the lounge, "it is to be expected. If there is anything I can do to help, anything, let me know."

She emphasised *anything* because she knew I was normally very opposed to people making a fuss over me. This time though, I knew I needed to just get straight to the crux of it.

"Right now, I need your opinion. My mother told me something... something frightening before she died."

Viv's eyelids were tense and drawn wide. Her pupils enlarged. She jolted as her phone buzzed in her hand, breaking her gaze. The phone tilted in her palm so she could make out the caller before proceeding to put it into her bag.

"Who's that?"

"It's no one important." Viv shuffled against the velvet corner settee, settling in for the revelations, horizontal creases plastered against her forehead. "What did your mum tell you?"

Her hands were back to cradling mine. Coffees sat untouched, growing cooler by the minute. Sweat began to bloom at my armpits.

"I think you just need to read it for yourself."

I passed Viv the letter and focused my attention on Barney's apricot fur and began stroking him more vigorously than normal. After several minutes, Viv laid the letter down against her thighs. Her features creased as if she were in pain. I wonder what I had looked like the first time I read the letter. To be a fly on that wall.

After what felt like an eternity, she finally spoke with a grit to her voice, like she was straining to speak. "I don't understand. Why would your mum leave this for you?"

Of all the first questions to come, this one I did not expect. "I don't know. I guess she felt afraid." I was clutching at straws, desperate to get to the more pertinent point. "What do you think I should do?"

Viv turned herself from my gaze then. She began staring at her hands, twisting them over in her lap. "Do you believe her?" Her words a whisper between us.

My body stiffened with the inquisition. How could she question my mother's character, and so soon after her death? The accusation almost winded me.

I finally found my voice, "How can I not, Viv? Why would she lie about something like this? She is my mum for crying out loud! She wouldn't leave me with this information if it wasn't true."

Slightly abashed, by the flush to her cheeks, Viv continued, "Where was the letter?"

"Stuffed inside a jacket of hers. One she said I could inherit. One she knew I'd find." Viv didn't say anything, so I went on, "I just can't wrap my head around the idea of my father being this alter-ego villain. *Who is he meant to have killed anyway? When was he meant to have done these things?* Was it before I was born, in his past?" The questions hummed in my brain.

Finally, Vivienne spoke - quietening my thoughts. "Listen, your mother could have been confused when she wrote this. The meds and chemo could have impacted her state of mind. I know your dad, Zoe. He is no killer!" Her tone was stern and forceful. She stared at me with lips curled inwards.

She didn't understand. I shook my head. "How well do you ever really know a person though? We see one version of our parents. The only side of my father I know is him *as a father*. Who he is behind closed doors, well that could be entirely different." I could see this got Viv thinking so I kept going, "I need to know the truth, Viv. Despite what my mother says, I can't leave this alone. I need to know if my father is what she says... a killer, but I can't do it on my own."

Viv's head bolted up to meet my gaze. "What do you want me to do?"

My stomach was doing summersaults.

I knew the journalist in her wouldn't be able to walk away from such a request. My mother didn't want me to investigate these allegations, but she said nothing about my newspaper-columnist-best-friend doing so.

"I'll see what I can do," Viv responded.

As I said, she was my absolute rock.

4

Zoe

In the days after my chat with Vivienne, I had to see my father, especially given that we would both be at Grace's funeral. Staying away from him after my mum died wasn't a plausible response. He'd suspect something to be amiss if I'd abandoned him without reason. Besides, some part of me still needed my father. I was so conflicted about how to react. Viv might be right. My mum could be mistaken, and I couldn't live with myself if I didn't give him a chance.

The funeral was hard. For most of the day, I stood or sat next to him. Both adorned in the only black clothes we owned, although physically together, we mourned separately. Alone. Silent. Not once did we utter a word about her to one another. How we missed her. How unfair it was that she was gone. The only interactions we had, were the condolences of friends and family. Like robots, we smiled and nodded to others' kindnesses. At the wake, we separated into our different social cliques, drowning our sorrows. I wasn't prepared for him to make a speech.

"I just want to say, thank you for being here today. I know Grace would be comforted by the outpouring of love that you have all shared with Zoe and me. It means the world to us."

I felt inclined, so I smiled at this notion, feeling the redness rise across my chest as all eyes stared at me, eager for my father to continue - curious to know what he'd say.

"Grace was the love of my life. As trivial as that phrase may sound, it really is true. She lit up every room she entered, and people just loved to be around her. She was funny, beautiful, and genuine. I don't want to dwell on the bleakness that was the last decade of her life. I want today to be about remembering Grace in her heydays! The Grace we all knew and cherished. To Grace!"

Through the surge of clinking glasses, Viv chirped up in my ear, "Christ, if he is a killer, he is one of the best actors going."

I followed Viv's gaze as it sized up my father. "How's the research going? Found anything yet?" I replied with a swig of wine.

"Well I didn't want to get into it here, but I think I've found something of interest. Come round to my place tomorrow, after the wake."

My skin tingled with anticipation and dread. "I can't wait until tomorrow, Viv. I know it looks unsympathetic, but I need to do this tonight. The not knowing is killing me."

Her eyebrows raised at my turn of phrase. I pushed my hands together in prayer and mimed 'please'.

"Okay, okay. I hear you. Let's just put things on the back burner for now and focus on your mum. She deserves a proper send-off." With that Viv lifted her glass, indicating me to do the same.

"To mum," I whispered, all the while contemplating what secrets Viv had uncovered.

Back at Viv's place, my tummy was in knots. I knew I'd need more alcohol in my system before embarking on the next part of our evening.

Without even uttering a word, Viv declared, "Wine is in the fridge, help yourself, and grab me a glass while I set up my laptop."

I sauntered over to her kitchen; an interior as put together as Viv. I cast my gaze across the clean, shiny surfaces with pops of cherry red accents from her designer kettle and toaster. The world could be coming to an end, and everything would still be neatly in its place.

My hands found the integrated fridge after a few attempts. I eagerly grabbed the entire bottle and two glasses before heading to her bedroom. One of the glasses slipped from my grasp and plummeted to the floor, shattering into jagged shards. Glancing my head round the doorway, I could see that Viv was firing up her laptop, focused and raring to go. Undeterred, she simply told me to clean it up later and grab another (less fancy) glass from her cupboard without breaking task.

"You ready?"

I poured myself a large glass of Pinot Grigio, inhaled the liquid courage and nodded.

"Okay, so it's not much. I've had a lot going on at work and could only do so much since our chat, but I think I'm on the right track. I started googling about murders in the area - actually found a website that tracks murders in your local area. Someone has set this up. It has a whole section dedicated to unsolved crime. You just type in your postcode, and it will generate a list of incidents within a ten-mile radius. I stretched the search area to include all of York, and started looking through the list, to see if anything jumped out." Viv tapped at her screen before revealing her finding. "Here - A woman, thirty-one years old, stabbed seven times, left for dead in Howardian Hills. No suspect. No witnesses. Found by dog walkers."

The case interested me, but I didn't see an association with my father, "What makes you think it has anything to do with my dad?" I asked, now pacing up and down her room.

"First of all, the park is only an eighteen-minute drive away. Second of all, the date."

My muscles turned rigid. "What about the date?"

"She was killed the day you were born, 12th January, 1987."

I sucked in my breath. My mother and I told the story of my birth to friends and family as an entertaining anecdote. A jibe in jest. Viv, in attendance at all my social events, must have heard the story a dozen times. Whenever anyone mentioned someone being late, or forgetting something, or making a blunder, my mother would interject, "Don't get me started! I've got the epitome as a husband! You should think yourself lucky. No one could find him! There I was, going into labour, and James was nowhere to be found. I'd woken up with soaked sheets, and the contractions were already intense. I rolled over to tell James and he wasn't in bed. We didn't have a mobile back then, so I went next door. Neighbours kindly took me to the hospital, and all the while I'm thinking - where the hell is he? I go through the entire labour on my own. I'm sitting there, holding Zoe, at that point unnamed, and in he walks, with a shopping bag, as if nothing was amiss. So I ask him, 'where have you been?' That's when he pulled out a pot of ice-cream and said we'd run out. During my pregnancy, I couldn't get enough of the stuff, so when he noticed we'd run out, he popped off to the off-license to restock. He said when he realised I must have gone into labour, he walked to the hospital. Figured labour took a while, and he'd make it in time! Men! It is safe to say that I've gone right off ice-cream!"

My father would laugh off the story, claiming he'd been slandered for being a doting partner trying to do a good deed. No one ever questioned his whereabouts or asked exactly how long he was gone, or why he went at such a ridiculous time.

I stood up a little straighter and aired my concerns, "My God. That is weird. Why have I never heard of this case?"

"The woman who died had no partner, was estranged from her family, and had no children that we're aware of. She has never been formally identified. No one knows who she is. I guess a middle-aged nobody wasn't big news back in the day. Isn't like now with social media. The newspaper headlines changed daily. Most people bought national news; the main stories were the big stories."

"I still think a local, mysterious murder like that would have hit Haxby. This could have been what started my mother's suspicions. If she did hear about it, wouldn't you suspect?"

"Possibly, or your mum could have still been in the hospital, or been busy with you - her new-born baby."

Whatever this was, it felt significant. There are coincidences and then there are coincidences. This felt personal. Coldness consumed my body. If this was my father's doing, why choose to murder someone on the day your daughter is about to be born? It was incredible of Viv to uncover it.

"I can't believe you found this, Viv. This is impressive stuff. It must have taken you hours. Thank you." I held her gaze.

"Anything I can do to help. What does it actually prove though?" she asked curiously.

"It makes my mother's claims plausible if nothing else. We need more though. Are there any similar crimes to this?"

"I don't know, as soon as I saw this one, I fixated on it. What would we look for next?"

I jumped into detective mode, thinking strategically. "Murderers are meant to have an MO right? Let's focus on the things this murder has."

I grabbed a pen and paper and start scribbling down notes for Viv to see. Weapon equals knife. Women. Lonely. Woods. York.

"When did your parents move to Haxby, do you know?" Viv queried.

I scratched my head, thinking. "They met in '79 in Ireland when my mum was visiting there. I think they married in '85 and moved to Haxby that same year. I don't know where they lived before then, or if they were even living together before they got hitched."

I was impressed by how much I could remember. I normally couldn't recall what I ate for breakfast.

"That's plenty for now. Let's focus on the stabbings of women in and around Haxby between 1985 and today." Anyone listening in on our conversation would think we were professionals. Or idiots.

"Won't the Police have done this exact same thing? Are we being silly?" Were we silly?

"Probably, but what else are we going to do?"

Viv was right. I couldn't *not* look into it. I was in too deep now. Going back to any sort of normal existence was out of the question.

"Sorry mum," I said, edging closer to Vivienne. "How do we search?"

"Good old Google."

5

Zoe

We searched for hours on various websites, even paying for access to some courtroom transcripts, but we just hit a brick wall. Tired of researching, I kept coming back to the story about the unidentified woman found in Howardian Hills. There was a sketch of her alongside the report, a girl with long, brunette hair and large, round eyes. Friendly eyes, I thought, but with heavy bags. She looked aged by life despite her short years that weren't far off mine.

She'd been stabbed in the neck and back. As if struck from behind unsuspectedly. Preyed upon. She wasn't sexually assaulted, or at least they hadn't said she was. The report included that she was in possession of drugs, and the idea of her not making major headlines suddenly made more sense. A lady on the fringes of society wasn't all that interesting. I suspected she was a runaway. Still, she was someone's daughter. Yet no one declared her missing. Could my father really be responsible? My skin prickled with uncertainty.

"I'll keep searching," Viv announced as I potted about making cups of coffee in a sleep-deprived haze.

"Don't, you've done enough. I've been thinking how crazy this all is. I shouldn't have even involved you. You have your own life to live, I don't want to drag you into this mess." I felt awful for how much I'd put on Viv. What would I even do with this information anyway?

"I really don't mind. It might sound twisted, but I had fun last night. We haven't had a sleepover in years! It feels good to help, to be of use."

"To what end though?" I asked. Although deep down, I knew exactly what she meant. Viv and I were bonding like sisters over this investigation. I no longer felt absorbed by my mother's death; I had a mission. A distraction. A very morbid distraction.

Viv's expressive eyebrows were back. "You've already broken one of your mother's wishes doing this. Are you going to break any more?"

I sighed, "I don't know what to do. If I up and leave, where would I go? Then there is you. I don't want to leave you. I like my life here. I like my shitty job. I like my little house. Besides, I have no savings to start again, even if I wanted to."

"So what about your dad? Are you going to...to accuse him? I need to know Zoe if you are because it might not be safe. I can come with you. Please tell me if you are!"

"No, absolutely not! I can't do that. Let's just keep looking for more information for now and regroup when we find something, then go from there," I instructed. "Mum said killings. Plural. There must be something else."

With that, I departed Viv's house and headed home. With each weighted stride, flashes of my life before my mother's death spiralled through my thoughts.

I remember one birthday, I think it was my tenth or eleventh, and my dad sat sulking in the living room. It wasn't unusual for him to not help out with party decorations or buffet prep, but he didn't move for the entirety of the day. It was like he couldn't see us. I hadn't thought about that day in so long. His sagging jowls and glazed eyes took on a sinister tone. I shook my head to quieten the scenes.

My cat was probably dying of starvation by now. As suspected, Barney proceeded to meow around my legs upon entry to my home. I flopped into bed after feeding him, ready to sleep for a hundred hours.

I must have only drifted off for a few minutes when my phone started to ring. Looking at my screen, I could see who was calling. It was my father.

"Hi love, where've you been? I've missed you," he pleaded as soon as I answered.

It felt so strange. A week ago this man was my world. Now, he was a stranger. A heavy feeling grew in the pit of my stomach.

"I'm so sorry. I've just been busy. I need to keep busy you know. It helps. How are you coping?" I tried to sound as normal as possible.

"I get that, I just feel like I've done something wrong. I didn't even get to say bye to you at the funeral. Is everything okay?"

He was dodging my question and going straight for the jugular.

I began to pull at the neck of my top. "You know what, I didn't feel well that night. I don't know if it was the booze or my nerves. Viv had to take me home." Can someone tell that you're lying over the phone?

"That's strange, because I went to your place, after the funeral, and you weren't there."

It dawned on me; he has a key for my place. He must have let himself in. The thought of him walking around my house, stalking, alone, sent shivers down my spine.

"When I say home, I mean Viv's home. I didn't want to be alone. You've just woken me from a nap, my mind is all over the place." I tried to say the last part with a yawn for effect.

"Right. Well as long as we're good. When can I see you next? You know you left mum's jacket here? I assume you you wanted it?"

Visions of him putting his grubby hands all over her things made my blood boil. I needed to calm down, play it cool. "Did I? I'll come over to get it and see you too. How about tomorrow after work? I could stop for tea if you like?" I tried to sound chirpier, aloof even.

"That would mean the world. It has been lonely around here. I think we need each other right now, don't you think?" Tears sprang from my eyes. I so desperately wanted him to not be a killer - to just be my father.

Images of my mother, father, and I sitting around a dining table came into view. It was on such an evening Grace announced she was sick. The world swept from under me in an instant. You expect your parents to be an anchor you can always rely on. To help you at every hurdle in life. Boy did I take that for granted. Tomorrow isn't a given. The day I learnt of my mother's illness was the day I was confronted with mortality. Then she got better, and I felt hopeful.

"Yes. I agree, I'll do better. See you tomorrow then. About 5 pm sound good?" I sounded so sincere. Really, I was just defeated.

"Perfect, I'll rustle up one of your favourites. Bye for now."

I put the phone down first before he could say his usual final words on a call... *love you*. Afterwards, I curled up under the duvet willing myself to sleep and wake from this nightmare.

6

Grace - Before

Dear diary,

The alarm woke me this morning, but I haven't been able to leave the bed. As soon as I heard it beep, I jolted upright and instantly regretted moving so fast.

My muscles still ache with pain. The cancer eats away at me. Every hour, every minute, every second, it grows and spreads. It's like living in a house with parasites you can never catch. Except the house is my own body. Some days, I yearn for death. To be free from the hurt. Then I remember, and there is nothing else I can think about. I never speak of it, but it is always there, caught at the back of my throat like a fly entangled in a spider's web. The lies. The betrayal.

I don't know what I find more crippling – the cancer or him.

7

Zoe

I must have slept for well over twelve hours. When I woke, it was almost time for me to rise for work. Turning my gaze out of my bedroom window, I could see raindrops seeping down the pane, smearing the outside world. There were streaks of silver highlighted by the streetlamp's dim glow and, between the falling dew, the concrete had that tell-tale sheen of wetness.

Of course, I didn't need to go to work. The home office said that I could take as long as I needed (although I doubt they meant with full pay). I stared at the ceiling, mulling over the idea, but then I promptly shut it down. I wanted to get back to *some* sort of normal. Whatever that may be. Besides, Viv would be back in the office, cracking York's finest stories wide open, and I couldn't exactly let her do all the work whilst I wallowed in self-pity.

She'd been working for The Press for a few years and loved it. Back when she first started it was a different story. When she almost quit, frustrated with the menial jobs of credits and TV guides, she came to me.

"I didn't do a journalist degree to end up writing the stuff no one cares about!" she complained, one balmy summer evening over Pimm's in a beer garden. "I'm a good writer Zoe, I could do so much more."

I hadn't seen her so hard-done-by since her last break-up at the end of University. Since then, she'd been practically celibate; completely and utterly focused on working up the ladder, but instead she was just staying put in one place.

My advice impressed even myself, "Listen, Viv, you're no quitter. I say you speak to your boss or the editor. Tell them you want to do something bigger. They aren't mind readers."

Personally, I avoided my colleagues as much as possible. I reckon if Viv and I hadn't been childhood friends, I'd be a complete and utter loner. Yet we did find one another. Like opposite ends of a magnetic, we stuck together and never let go. A rare friendship, as precious as a pearl hidden in the depths of the ocean; Viv was the sister that I never had.

Vivienne took my advice, and it paved the way for her promotion. They appreciated how gutsy she was. From that, she covered news that made the front page.

When I first saw her name printed in black and white, *Words by Vivienne Cooper*, it filled me with the same pride of a dotting parent. My best friend was realising her dreams. I'm just glad that she hadn't chased the huge titles within the big smoke. Thankfully, her success hadn't changed her one bit. She was still as caring as ever. In fact, the older we got, the more protective she became.

Caught up in my daydream of reminiscing, I'd missed the sunrise.

"The early bird catches the worm aye, Barney."

I'd become that person. The type that talked to their pets. I wasn't an actual cat lady as I only had the one, but if a husband never came along then I would happily adopt that title.

Stumbling out of bed, I forced myself into the shower, letting the warm water wash away the night from my aching skin and melt away all of my worries., if only for a brief time. It cocooned my body with its caressing touch like a mother lion licking the wounds of her child. A quivering grin stretched across my face for this was the closest thing that I had to intimacy. The only thing.

It took me a while to peel myself away from the flowing embrace, but that didn't stop me arriving to work before anyone else, hair still damp.

I stared at my computer screen, a blue, blaring light amongst the grey room, and my fingers itched to type what my head was telling me not to. Self-restraint was never my strong suit. Before I knew it, I was googling murders.

There must be something we're missing, I pondered.

Web page after web page, eyes scanning line after line, nothing made a connection. Obsessively scrolling, my coffee grew cold and untouched. Then I saw it.

Six chilling crimes that shook York.

I clicked on the link and continued to read.

The notorious New Year's Eve York murder unsolved for ten years.

At the time the article had been written it was 2010, five years ago. They'd broadcasted to mark the anniversary on BBC's Crimewatch, in an attempt to gain new witnesses, but nothing had come to light. Like the previous case, there was no forensic evidence or CCTV. This time, the woman, Jane Powel, had initially survived before succumbing to her injuries.

Jane Powel, a sex worker from York, was left to die in the streets of Overton in the early hours of the morning on Friday 31st December, 2000. Her attacker stabbed her twelve times...

It was the location of those stab wounds that sent alarm bells ringing in my ears and a rush of heat to my cheeks.

Her attacker stabbed her twelve times in her back and neck, marginally missing any major arteries.

My eyes flittered between the words too quickly to comprehend what I was actually reading. Gripping the screen, I steadied myself and reread the text in full.

Ultimately, her injuries proved fatal, but not before Miss Powel could describe her assailant. Constable Henry Walker, who was the first officer on the scene, took a statement from Miss Powel. From this description, a photofit was generated. The photofit failed to provide any successful leads in the case. To this day, no one has been arrested for the crime.

I forced my shaking hand to click on the drawing based on her description. What first struck me was the similarity to my father, but there were some discrepancies too. Squinting at the picture, the man before me had thick, brown hair like my father's, but it was wavier. His jawline wasn't as broad, but to me, his eyes were a match. Piercing aqua-blue eyes that stood out against olive skin, tanned from years of working outdoors in construction. *Was it him?*

To help answer that question, I needed to know what my father was up to New Year's Eve that year.

People had a good recollection of 2000 with it being the turn of a new century. I remembered moments myself. We were at a party at my Aunt's house. I'd have been about thirteen years old. I recall watching the countdown on the telly, pulling poppers, and cheering. I think we all danced in a circle to Auld Lang Syne, and we watched in awe as the night sky filled with dazzling fireworks. That's it. I can't even say who exactly was there. I knew who would though. I needed to speak to Aunt Caitlyn.

8

Zoe

On my lunch break, after minutes of rehearsing in my head, I decided to make the call. After a couple of rings, her cheery voice answered, "Zoe dear, how are you holding up?"

"Okay, thanks. I'm actually back at work today. Fancied the distraction. How are you?"

Caitlyn was my mum's sister. They could have been twins they sounded so alike. I braced myself for it, gripping the phone tight.

"I...I have my moments as we all do. Something happens and I get that urge to call your mother, and then I remember," I could hear her voice breaking as she spoke. Tears welled up in my eyes at her words. I had to dig deep to keep pushing on.

"I know exactly what you mean. That is kind of why I'm calling you. I was looking through photos of mum and I came across that epic New Year's Eve party you did back in 2000. Do you remember it?"

I hoped it sounded believable. Deep down, a part of me wanted this conversation to just be that - a trip down memory lane – a simple conversation with my auntie about my mother.

"Oh yes! Gosh, that must have been about fifteen years ago. It was some party. Grace was so drunk! Mind you, so was I. What a night. We thought we had our whole lives ahead of us. Five years later she was diagnosed. Our world as we knew it fell apart."

The pit in my stomach deepened, and I swallowed my tears. "I know. Life can be so unfair...that's why I'm trying to focus on my mother at her brightest you know? How was she at the party? Was she... happy?" my voice shook as I spoke.

"She was radiant. The belle of the ball. I remember she wore this strappy, red dress and matching heels. She really was a knockout. We laughed and danced. You, Darcey and Vivienne were giggling in the corner."

Darcey was Caitlyn's daughter, my cousin. I felt a pang of guilt as I realised I had barely spoken to her at the funeral. Instead, I was focused on *him*. At my mother's funeral, I was focused on *him*.

"And my father? Where was he?"

"James? Well in all honesty darling he didn't stay for midnight. Your mother and father argued that night. I have no idea what it was about. I just vividly recall your father storming out, and that's when Grace began necking the prosecco. According to your mum, they made up the next day."

My hand reached for my throat as if protesting. I fought against my instincts. "Do you know what time he left?"

"No, sorry dear, I don't. It was a long time ago."

When I didn't reply, couldn't, she asked a question that nearly broke me. "Is everything alright?"

She worried, like a mother, like my mother. My heart sank. Physically, it weighed me down like a lead ball between my ribs.

"I just wondered, that's all," my voice just a whisper. "Thanks so much for revisiting old times with me Aunt Caitlyn. I have to get back to work now. I'll be sure to catch up with you and Darcey soon."

After we said our goodbyes and best wishes, I didn't know how I'd get through the rest of the shift with a clear head. My mind whirled.

Two murders.

Both times my father went missing. This felt very real now. I think before this point I had my doubts, but now I felt certain. Everything was sliding into place. The late nights, the arguments, the slammed doors. They came rushing back like a tidal wave. The force was so strong, I felt physically sick. I jumped up from my desk, knocking the remnants of my coffee over my keyboard.

"Are you alright?" I heard as I bolted to the toilet, just in time for bile to spill into the bowl.

Beth had followed me in. "I think you should go home Zoe, get some rest. Maybe it is too soon for you to be back."

I took the afternoon off, and as if no time had passed, reconvened my earlier state by lying back in bed. The unmade duvet had a sickly-sweet smell, like it hadn't dried properly when I put it on. Unable to muster the strength to change them, I just endured the stench, staring at the ceiling.

A thought haunted my mind, robbing me of sleep; *How on earth was I meant to go for tea at my father's tonight?*

9

Grace – Before

Dear Diary,

When I first met James, I was on holiday with my family visiting Ireland – back when my parents were together. I'd been on a walk in the wild and windy foothills, and we'd taken shelter in a cosy pub, just as the heavens opened. Nestled in the corner, I sat with my sister and mother. My father placed our drinks order at the bar when I saw him – a broad, distinguished-looking boy laughing with a group of friends. He had an enigmatic, raspy laugh and impeccable white teeth. His fingers kept combing his long hair back off his face. Absorbed in conversation, he sat hunched over his pint glass. At sixteen, I'd dabbled with the odd boyfriend, but I was yet to find someone that kept me interested. As I sat by the roaring fire, in that idyllic country pub, I just knew. He was the one.

Confidence hadn't ever been an issue for me. If I had anything going for me back then, it was my relentless determination. When I saw him motion to the bar for another round, I asked my dad if I could buy a drink. Oblivious to my real intentions, he accepted with a shrug and passed me some cash. The rain showed no signs of slowing, and the bar was in eyesight but not earshot. As soon as I ordered, I took the plunge.

I asked if he needed a hand, eyeing up the row of ale in front of him. He told me that carrying lots of glasses was his speciality in this thick Irish accent before asking where I was from. I pointed to the group of people who sat sleepily in their seats and told him of my family holiday. We chatted about England some more, he'd always wanted to go himself. He recommended places of interest to see during my stay in Ireland. Then out of the blue, he asked if I wanted him to be my tour guide.

It didn't take long for my parents to agree to our meet up. We spent most of that holiday together after that fateful conversation in the pub. After that, we stayed in touch, wrote letters, and spoke on the telephone for hours at a time. Then he got a job in England. He was some years older than me and had been working for a contractor in Ireland that had gone bust. There were lots of building trade to be had in York at the time, so he managed to snap up work easily. Fast forward a couple of years and we are shacked up married. Those years were blissful. Perfect even. The happiest of my life. I couldn't imagine anything coming between us. Somehow, I was completely wrong.

10

Zoe

I'd decided to cycle. Living in the centre of York meant that owning a bike was integral. I adored living in the heart of this beautiful, ancient city, but some of the cobbled roads were almost impassable. Attempting to navigate a car through lanes that were once made for horse and carriage proved perilous. Moreover, I needed to feel the wind on my skin.

I pedalled hard through the hustle and bustle. York cathedral pierced the sky overhead. To anyone looking, I was simply a girl on her bike when in actual fact, I was a girl with a secret.

I approached my old home gingerly, The Stranglers blaring in my ears. I stopped still at the front door. Was it fear that prevented me from knocking? I could practically hear the thud of my heart over the clank of No More Heroes. The door opened before me.

He was standing there.

"Come on in then, you'll catch a chill."

I followed him into the hallway, slowly taking my earbuds out and shoes off. I wanted to waste as much time as possible. Inevitably, I made my way into the kitchen, my senses on tenterhooks. The tang of homemade lasagne filled the air. Red wine, already opened, sat expectantly on the side.

"Pour a glass," he offered with a tea towel in his hand, "I'm just about to dish up."

At the table, I glanced over all the hard work that he'd gone to. Garlic bread. A rocket salad. Napkins. He'd never been this domesticated when mum was alive. It felt alien. *He* felt alien.

"I thought you'd forgotten about your oul fella," he said with a sheepish smirk. Oul fella is an Irish term for father. I used to call him that as a kid. Back when his Irish slang fascinated me. Back when I wasn't afraid of him.

The plate of food looked piping hot. I felt disappointed that I couldn't dive straight in and fill my mouth to avoid talking. The only other option was to talk about anything other than what actually consumed me.

"I'm sorry I've been off lately," I began while taking a piece of garlic bread and blowing on it. "I went back to work today but had to leave after a few hours. I don't think I'm quite ready to pick up where I left off."

He reached out to me then and placed his hand on mine. His expression, filled with love, bore into my soul, paralysing me to my seat.

"That's good love," he said. "I think you should take it slow. I know I am. That reminds me. I put that jacket you were after on the sofa. That's the one, isn't it?"

I followed his pointing finger. There, laid over the back of the cream sofa, was my mother's jacket. My jacket. Just the sight of it made me flush with nerves.

Why would he parade it around like that?

I had a horrible thought that he knew about the letter all along. Surely, he'd have done away with it.

"Yep, that's the one, thanks." I wiped the crumbs from my mouth as I continued, "Remind me to take it on my way out."

"How is Vivienne?" he asked, eyes dropping to his plate.

"Viv? She's okay. She's been a big support, as always. Why'd you ask?"

"Just curious, that's all, a little like you earlier."

There was a sudden switch in his tone.

"Aunt Caitlyn called, she said that you rang her. Something about bringing up a past New Year's Eve party - completely out of the blue."

Anxiety radiated from my body. I was sure he could smell it on me as I wrung my hands under the table.

"Just rehashing old memories of mum that's all. It's nice to hear about times before she fell ill."

I spoke into my food, not wanting to meet his eyes. Had I avoided them all evening?

"You know you can always ask me about things like that?" he said with a slurp of his wine.

"I know I can," I said, pushing pasta back and forth with my fork.

The real question was, did I dare?

The silent air hung heavy between us, an invisible forcefield fuelled by suspicion and distrust.

"That night, the night that you asked your aunt Caitlyn about..." My jaw slacked ajar, awaiting his next sentence. "...your mother and I fought, as we did many nights."

"You argued? I don't remember you fighting."

"We tried our best to wait until you were in bed. We wanted to shield you from the upset."

The lucid dream from nights ago soared to the forefront of my mind. *Was it a suppressed memory after all?*

Waiting, I watched as my father continuously spun his gold wedding band round the base of his finger. "I'd come to Caitlyn's New Year's Eve party from the pub with some workmates. Grace was up in arms about it. Accused me of being with another woman."

My breathing haltered. "Why would she think that?"

My father's hand covered his mouth, his lids blinked rapidly. Through his muffles I could just make out his reply, "I have no idea."

Was my whole upbringing one big deception? The thought exploded in my chest, robbing me of breath for dizzying moment.

"I've got a headache coming on," my hand rose to my knitted brow. "Best not to overdo it."

I couldn't help but notice my father's disappointed glare. I watched as it softened in the candlelight into the face that I had grown up with. The face that I once recognised as my dad.

My chair pushed backwards as I stood, creating an uncomfortable, jarring screech. I quickly thanked him for dinner before turning to leave. His heavy footsteps followed me to the front door, a drumming beat to my racing heart.

"Don't forget this." He passed me the jacket I'd left strewn out on my mother's bed. The same jacket that'd had a ticking timebomb enclosed within its inside pocket. I took it from his grasp and draped it carefully over my arm.

We both stared at the empty cloth, thinking of her. Even as I left the house, I didn't turn back to see if my father was watching me from the doorway. I kept my eyes unwaveringly fixed on the sacred fabric cradled in my arms.

When I arrived back home, I punched through my contacts in search of Viv's number. I needed to bring her up-to-speed.

"I found another murder, Viv." No need for pleasantries.

"What? I thought I was the award-winning journalist?" She genuinely sounded offended.

"Well looks like you've got competition. So, are you coming over? I need my sidekick."

I don't know if it was the adrenaline of being with my father face-to-face, or knowing I was making headway, but a strange swell of giddiness flew through my veins.

"Give me ten minutes. Have the wine ready."

She read my mind.

Viv was an excellent timekeeper. In ten minutes, she was flying through my door eager to know more.

"Let's do this." She ushered us into the lounge where I'd already set up the laptop on the Jane Powel report. I watched in anticipation while she read, inhaling the scent of cool, night air that had waded in with her arrival. My tapping fingers strummed against my thighs; I craved her acknowledgement - her alliance.

"Interesting," she finally proclaimed.

I wanted clarity. "Interesting because... I'm on to something?"

"It depends. What was James doing that night? Do you know?"

"That's where things get really interesting. I called my aunt, who hosted a party that New Year. She says my father left before midnight after an argument with my mum."

My eyes widened and my brows lifted. I turned out my palms, waiting for her reply.

"Wow, Zoe...this is getting serious now. You have to stay away from him until we decide what to do about all this."

My face flushed. *Was I so naive?* "I've already been to see him, earlier today. He invited me over for tea."

I dodged the pillows as Viv threw them at me.

"Zoe! What did I say? I'd go with you. At the very least you should have informed me, so I could make sure you came home."

The sense of playfulness dissipated. "You think he'd hurt me?"

Zoe simply shrugged and sighed. That was a yes then.

"What should I do?"

I knew what she'd say, I just didn't want to be the first one to say it.

"I think we need to go to the police." The inner corners of her mouth pulled downwards as she spoke as if they soured against her talk. "We have the letter, two murders, and two accounts of James being unaccounted for during such events. Your right, it doesn't look great."

"Come with me?" I asked while nudging her fondly on the shoulder.

"Of course, I'm your sidekick, remember?"

That night, we organised when we'd head for the station. Zoe was covering a story the next day but would be free after work. We knew we might be questioned for some time so planned on grabbing a bite to eat before. Somewhere quick. A drive-thru.

After we'd polished the wine off, we said our goodbyes. I didn't have work in the morning, so instead of rolling into bed, I decided to stay up and watch Netflix. A crime documentary came up on my recommended list. Was my laptop listening to me? A thought passed my mind then. One day, my father could be the centre of one of these shows. What would I say if I were interviewed? Would I show forgiveness? Would I visit him in jail? Would I still love him? It was pointless considering such possibilities. First things first, I needed to prove that he was guilty.

11

Grace – Before

Dear diary,

This diary has become a form of therapy for me. I didn't realise how much I needed to divulge, how much I needed to purge. When I cannot sleep, like I can't now, the hurt too strong to shake, the only thing to bring me some form of relief is writing. The truth is, I wish I could rewrite my life, but that is beyond me. All I can do is consider what happened, and where things went so terribly wrong.

As soon as I fell pregnant, James became distant. Cold. He would go through periods of barely talking to me and working late to being overwhelmingly caring and thoughtful. As my belly grew, the loving side of James diminished, and a seed of resentment flourished within me.

Every time he snapped at me or complained about the house or our finances, that resentment would grow. I tried so hard to crush it. We'd go on trips away and have moments that reminded me of the boy that I fell in love with. Then I'd hear him sneaking back into the house, late at night, reeking of sin. Thoughts would consume my mind. Was it my fault? Did I push him away?

12

Zoe

I expected the building to look foreboding, intimidating. The North Yorkshire Police Station reminded me of flats or offices. It sat sandwiched between a carpark and streets lined with leafy sycamores. The brickwork matched the surrounding houses, the only difference was the size of the place. It was a big station. Out of the two options in York, we decided on the main, central base. Figured they'd have more manpower. More resources.

Upon walking up to the entrance, I couldn't shake my nerves.

"Why is it that I feel like I'm the one in trouble?" I queried.

"Police have that effect on people," Viv responded, calmly. "We have nothing to fear."

"What do we say when we reach reception?"

This part we hadn't discussed.

"Let me do the talking." Viv squeezed my hand briefly, before sauntering headstrong towards the lady behind the desk.

"Can I help you?" The receptionist behind the desk was smiley and approachable. I instantly felt more at ease.

"We need to speak to someone about a couple of old cases. We believe we have important information to share." Brief, succinct, and to the point. Viv must be badass when conducting interviews.

The lady behind the desk widened her eyes. I guess they don't get these types of visitors often. "Right. If I could get the names of the cases in question?"

I looked around to see if anyone could overhear.

"Jane Powel. The other female was never identified."

"And you are?"

"I'm Vivienne Cooper," she gestured to herself and then over to me, "this is my friend Zoe Murphy."

The lady scribbled the names on a piece of paper and advised that we take a seat while she found an investigating officer.

We must have waited only five minutes when a short, clean-cut officer approached us, arm outstretched. His hazel eyes darted across from Viv to me.

"I'm DC Wilde. Which one of you is Vivienne and which one is Zoe?"

"I'm Vivienne." Viv shook DC Wilde's hand firmly. I noticed the dark hairs on the back of his palm.

"And I'm Zoe," I responded with my hand loosely enclosed within DC Wilde's grasp.

"Let's find a nice, quiet room where we can talk, shall we?"

I felt like a schoolgirl being sentenced to the headmaster's office as we navigated the long corridors. My hands began to shake uncontrollably by my sides. My legs wanted to buckle underneath me with the weight of our ordeal. I knew it was the adrenaline, my fight or flight responses kicking in. I told myself, I was going to fight.

We stepped into a neutral room with an oval wooden desk and four chairs. There was a clinical smell to the room, reminiscent of polish cleaner. Opposite, sat a female officer with a folder, pen, and paper in front of her. As we came nearer, she stood to greet us.

"My name is DI Jones. I hope you don't mind me sitting in on this discussion."

Viv and I shook our heads in unison.

"Can we get you anything before we start?" She tucked a loose strand of golden hair behind her ear as she spoke. Her frame was slight, but I could tell by the way she held herself that she took no prisoners.

"Water please," Viv answered.

Did it look bad that I let Viv do all the talking?

DC Wilde left the room and re-entered with two cups of water, fresh from the cooler. "Our receptionist informs us you have information regarding some cold cases. Would it be okay if I record this conversation in case you have anything valuable to offer?"

"Of course, we don't mind." Viv didn't need to check with me. She knew I'd just be happy to get straight to it. My throat felt so parched already. I almost finished the cup of water in a single gulp.

"Before we begin, can you state for the recording your full names and connection with the case?"

After reinstating our names, Viv turned straight to me. This was my cue. All eyes fell upon my face.

"Viv is my best friend, she's only here for moral support really. I'm here because... I think my father is a... murderer. I have reason to suspect he killed a woman back in 1987, in Howardian Hills... and Jane Powel in 2000."

As the officers regarded one another, I felt on edge, exposed. A sense of powerlessness radiated across my core. There was something deeper too. Something lying in wait at the pit of my stomach, making me nauseous. Guilt? Fear? The worry of what this admission could set into motion struck every muscle in my body. If I'd have been standing, my body would have surely succumbed and crumpled in a heap on the floor. I took a deep breath and swallowed my anxiety, waiting for their judgement.

"That's a serious allegation, Zoe. What makes you think your father committed those crimes?" DI Jones seemed to be taking the lead on the questioning. Was it because we were females too?

I reached tentatively inside my bag and pulled out the letter. As I shakily handed it over to DI Jones, she announced what was happening – for the tape.

"My mother wrote me this before she died. Cancer. Nearly two weeks ago."

I filled them in on where I found it, before outlining the rest of our research. Darting glances flew across the room. Why did no one seem alarmed by the information? It was my world that had been shattered. My sense of reality had been warped. When no one spoke, I unexpectedly slammed my hands on the table, demanding their feedback.

"Don't you think it looks suspicious that he went missing on the same nights that two women wound up dead? Especially after what my mum wrote?"

This time DC Wilde broke the silence. "It is certainly something we are going to have to look into. However, I need to tell you. These cases have no physical evidence. No witnesses. It is going to be incredibly hard to prove anything. I've been in this job a long time, and I don't want to see either of you get your hopes up."

"Even with the letter? Isn't that evidence?"

DI Jones leaned in and held my hands. "If we can prove it is written by your mother it certainly warrants an inquiry, but alone, it doesn't show culpability."

I felt shameful then. Was all this for nothing?

"Listen, until we speak to your father, we don't think it is safe to visit him. If he is dangerous, he could be angry with your statement."

My eyes flashed at DC Wilde. "You aren't going to tell him it was me who ratted him in, are you?"

"No, no. We won't mention you directly, but the evidence of the letter may do the talking for us. We will try and just focus on gathering testimony for his whereabouts on the nights in question, but if he isn't cooperative, it is the only leverage that we have."

I bit my lip hard, thinking. *What have I done? I want him caught if he is guilty. This is potentially worse. If he isn't convicted, where does that leave me and my relationship with my father?*

My palms were getting incredibly sweaty. Sensing my turmoil, Viv's soothing hand tapped my thigh.

"She can stay with me for as long as it takes, officers. When will you bring him in?"

"Let us know the address and we will be over there later today."

As they spoke, I started to feel odd. My brain felt heavy like sludge, and I could sense the colour draining from my face. Visions of my future life with my father flashed through my head. I would be forced to live perpetually in silence, without resolution. Without retribution. I couldn't let that happen.

"Zoe...Zoe...are you alright?"

All of a sudden, the corners of my vision were blurring. I couldn't keep a steady rhythm with my breath.

"I... think... I'm... having... a... panic... attack."

Viv coached me through my breathing, trying to calm me down. "Count, breathe in for five, breathe out for five. That's it, nice and steady. You're okay."

DC Wilde and DI Jones comforted me with compliments. "It is so brave of you to speak with us today. No matter what happens, we won't let anything bad happen to you or your friend."

Finally, my breathing steadied. I was too embarrassed to look directly at anyone. "Thanks," was all I could muster.

I managed to sign some documents and let Viv say our farewells. The thought of having to go back to the station for any follow-up questions left a sour taste in my mouth. All I wanted to do was hide under a rock until all of this was all over.

13

Grace - Before

Dear diary,

The day I dwell on, the day I cannot cleanse from my skin, steals my mind. The closer I get to the end, the more it rises its ugly head.

That day, I asked Caitlyn to babysit and decided to follow him. I wanted to know, once and for all what he was up to and what was driving him away from his family.

I borrowed a friend's car and found him driving around the known red-light district in the area. Shrouded in darkness, I witnessed him cruising for sex. After several minutes, he pulled up to a hooker and they exchanged words. Soon after, she got into his car, and they sped off. I caught up with them and parked far enough away to remain unseen. I could just make out the explicable act unfolding in the back seat. Bile rose in my throat. It was a level of disgust and hate that I had never felt before in my life, and I am convinced it was the moment my cancer erupted.

Of course, I confronted him about it. That's when the arguing turned nasty. Violent. The truth was, behind closed doors, we were animals to each other. James and me. Sometimes, I was worse than him. I can't pinpoint exactly where the darkness in me came from, but once I started, I couldn't stop.

14

Zoe

Viv and I lay next to each other under the hum of her bedroom light. We hadn't spoken much since we returned to her house. I loved how easy things were around Viv. Effortless. Sometimes, we didn't need to talk. When I did need to get something off my chest though, she was there, all ears.

"Why wait until she was dead?" I murmured.

"...I don't know."

"All my life my mum wanted to protect me. Then she leaves me with this shit to sort out all on my own?"

It wasn't a direct question, but the accusatory nature in my voice was undeniable. I was angry. No two ways about it.

"Grace loved you. I guess she felt guilty leaving you without telling you the truth," she said, turning her head to face mine. "People call it a death bed confession."

"You heard the police. If they can prove the letter was written by my mother, she was a witness. She could have made the difference here. My dad is just going to lie to the police. How can I go on, knowing this about him?"

"Zoe..." Viv's face changed in the half-light. Her lips pouted outwards, and her brows drew closer. Her mouth opened and then closed, struggling to continue.

"Yes?" I willed.

Her head shook and her brows loosened. "We don't know anything for a fact, Zoe. Neither of us does."

"That's even worse. Am I just expected to go on playing happy families, never knowing if my father is or isn't a serial killer? What if there are more, Viv? More murders we just don't know about yet? We haven't even looked into Ireland."

Tears sprang from my eyes, but I held them back.

"Let's not get worked up again. There is absolutely nothing we can do at this moment. Let the police do their job. Tomorrow I'll call in sick. You won't be alone."

Her hand rubbed my shoulder comfortingly, sending a tear down my cheek. She wiped it away before I could.

"For now, I think we need a laugh. Let's binge-watch a comedy sketch, and I'll make us some tea."

"Thanks, that sounds perfect," I muttered.

I didn't need a man in my life with Viv. Every time I felt like crumbling she kept me whole. *What would I ever do without her?*

15

Grace Before

Dear diary,

When the moment finally came for me to take back control over my life, I allowed all of the built-up anguish to explode. I had planned on confronting her, scaring her, but the prostitute wouldn't have it. She lunged at me, threatening me! I don't even remember pulling the knife from my coat. It all happened so fast. The recollection plays out with the same mist of red that descended upon me that evening.

I remember how my hand shivered as I clutched the knife. The prostitute laid face down motionless on the grass. Blood pooled around her neck, spilling on to the floor. Her gargles still echo in my mind, and I can still taste bile at the thought.

I didn't know how much Caitlyn had seen or heard from the car until she approached me from behind, hissing my name.

I told her not to look, begged her, but she knew what I'd done. I asked her to return to the car, and at that moment Zoe kicked hard against my stomach. The trauma settled in. Only hours later, I'd wake from my sleep and go into labour.

Caitlyn kept her word. She never did tell anyone about the night that I decided to confront the whore James was shagging, yet again. We never discussed it even to each other. It was as if it never happened. The news reports fizzled out and people forgot. The woman was never even identified. I'd been sure to take all her identification with me. They lurk in the watery depths of the River Ourse, along with the knife I used to stab her. It was only by chance that some stalker committed a very similar crime to a woman named Jane Powel in Overton. Distancing my association even further.

When Zoe was born it was like I too was born again. The horror of the night had been replaced by the magnificent joy of my daughter. In my head, my real life started the day I became a mother.

All my attention was on Zoe, my Zoe. I couldn't imagine my life without her in it. The thought was paralysing at times. I'd wake up in the night and run to her crib, just to check that she was still breathing. I'd agonise over her every move. James *was* a good father. He was incredibly hands-on and attentive.

As you would expect, something had changed between him and me. The sheer business of life distracted us from our problems for a while. Then karma caught up with me.

When I was diagnosed, the first time, my illness affected James. Overnight, he returned to his former self. Gentle, soft, and sweet. The affairs seemed to have ended, and I had bigger things to worry about. Ironically, the cancer brought a lot of goodness to our lives. We made time to be together as a family and make memories. As my condition improved and the cancer went into remission, I thought that we'd made it through the worst of it and come out stronger than ever. How naive I was.

16

Zoe

That morning, I woke to the sound of Viv on the phone with work. True to her word, she was faking an illness to stay with me. I got out of bed and flicked the kettle on, wanting to offer her a token of kindness.

"Coffee?" I asked as she finished her conversation.

"Please," she said as she nodded and inched closer, phone still clutched in her hand. "Listen, I had a phone call early this morning from DC Wilde. He spoke with your father yesterday and wants to tell us how it went. Get dressed and we'll head on over, yeah?"

My hands rested dead on the coffee mug.

"Is he in custody?"

Viv sighed, "...They had to let him go, Zoe. He was cooperative, and they had nothing to hold him."

The kettle rattled as the water hit boiling.

"So he didn't confess then? What is there to talk about?"

"Let's find out exactly how the conversation went at the station. It is the least we can do after DC Wilde and DI Jones followed up on our meeting yesterday." There was an edge to Viv's voice. Whose side was she on?

"No. I'm not going. I'm not leaving this house. My father has a key to my home. He knows I had something to do with all this and he's out there...roaming the streets...free!"

Viv stood with both her hands on the kitchen countertop, head dangling between. "Zoe, they don't think your father is the killer."

I couldn't believe my ears. Yesterday, Viv was ready to go into battle for me. Now, we faced our own standoff.

Viv's features softened. "They say he doesn't fit the photofit from the Jane Powel case, and Jane never mentioned an Irish accent, something that would have stood out."

The spoon in my hand dropped onto the countertop, and I spun around to face Viv square on, my feet resolutely planted in place.

"I saw that photofit and the eyes matched. Anyone can fake an accent. Don't you think a murderer would cover that up, to avoid being identified?" Doesn't she think I'd already considered the accent thing?

Vivienne backed off and began gathering her things. "Listen, I'm going, with or without you. We started this journey, and now we need closure. I need to know what he said." Her hand hovered over the front door's handle. "Are you coming?"

I turned Viv down a second time. I just couldn't bring myself to go to the station again and listen to their apparent incompetence. If my father saw me leave Viv's he'd know where I was holding up. *Surely, it was safer to lie low.*

17

Zoe

I didn't know how long Viv would be, so at first, I wasn't worried. She left for the station about 9:30 am. I clocked the time when I resumed our comedy antics from the night before. By midday, I figured she'd decided to pick up lunch on her way home. At 1 pm my phone started ringing, sending me running across the room.

"Viv? Where are you?" I answered, breathless.

"Sorry, it's DC Wilde. Is everything alright?"

"I was expecting Viv back by now, has she left yet?"

"I was calling to see if you knew where Vivienne was, we were expecting her some time ago. When did she leave?"

"Around 9:30 am. It couldn't have taken her longer than half an hour to reach you."

Silence.

"And you haven't heard from her since?" The air of concern was absolute.

"No, I've texted her, but I figured she couldn't use her phone at the station. She never made it?"

"No. Zoe, is there anywhere else she would have gone? Do you think she would consider approaching your father by herself at all?"

The very idea made my blood run cold. Would Viv go to see my father, alone?

Tears trickled down my face without me holding back, "...I...I don't know."

"Sit tight. We will send someone round. Check the place out. We'll find her Zoe. We'll find her."

It turns out, they were wrong.

When I first met Viv, I was just five years old. We started school together. From the minute I saw her, I loved her. As a kid, Viv was so sparky and creative. All the girls wanted to be her, and all the guys wanted to date her. I was like a moth to a flame. No one ever came between us. Until now.

All afternoon I crouched by the phone, waiting. I didn't eat, didn't sleep. I didn't move an inch – couldn't. I was no longer aware of myself. All I could think about was Viv. Where was she? Was she hurt?

Outside, the sky grew a deep marine, and I watched as shadows slowly floated across the timber floors. In the distance, the city buzzed with life; engines roared, birds sang, and people gossiped.

When the police updated me on the situation, I knew I'd never see Vivienne again. Something deep inside of me just knew.

"We've spoken to family, work – no one has seen or heard from her," they informed me.

My eyes closed heavy. My heart sank. "And my father?"

"She's not with him. He has an alibi, Zoe. He's been at work all morning. We've filled a missing person's report and will continue checking nearby CCTV and cash machines. Did she say anything, anything at all about leaving town?"

How can someone just vanish? They made no sense. "Viv would never just leave me without telling me where and why," saliva spluttering from my mouth as I spoke. "She's my best friend. I know her. This has to have something to do with my father. The day after we submit evidence, condemning him, Vivienne goes missing. Don't you think that's strange DI Jones?"

After a few awkward seconds, she replied, "I'm sorry Zoe. We will continue searching. Viv might likely turn up. Are you able to stay at her house in case she returns? Will you let us know if you hear from her?"

"Yes, of course. I really hope you're right."

"If you need us, Zoe, if something happens, anything, you call us. Okay?"

"Yep...thanks." I tried not to sound disheartened, I knew DI Jones was only trying to be sympathetic. I just couldn't understand how any of this was happening, and it felt like nobody was helping.

After the call with the police, I arranged for my neighbour to feed Barney while I stayed at Vivienne's place. I couldn't face food, but my throat longed for spirits. A bottle of gin perched elegantly atop a gold drinks trolley. Forgoing a glass, I glugged a quarter in one sip. My throat scorched with the heat. It tasted acrid. Harsh. Good.

Beyond the kitchen, the bed beckoned. Without hesitation, I ambled in, gin bottle in hand, and cocooned myself in Vivienne's sheets, contemplating how on earth I let any of this happen.

In a drunken haze, I reached for my mobile and watched through rolling eyes as my phone rang. Then I heard his voice. I ignored his greeting and slurred against the phone, "Where is she?"

"I don't know, Zoe. Come home, please. I can—"

"You are *lying* to me. You've been lying to me for a long time haven't you?" I snarled. "I know you have done something. If you ever loved me, you would tell me what you have done!"

The phone beeped against my ear – *call ended*. I stared at the mobile in my trembling hand, building with rage, and launched it into the air. I didn't flinch when it smatters onto the floor. I remained curled up in a ball, reeling from the exchange, trying to understand what it meant.

18

Zoe

Do not stand at my grave and weep
I am not there. I do not sleep.
I am a thousand winds that blow.
I am the diamond glints on snow.
I am the sunlight on ripened grain.
I am the gentle autumn rain.
When you awaken in the morning's hush
I am the swift uplifting rush
Of quiet birds in circled flight.
I am the soft stars that shine at night.
Do not stand at my grave and cry;
I am not there. I did not die.
By Mary Elizabeth Frye[1]

Without a body, there could be no poem more fitting for Vivienne's funeral. Seven years had passed since Viv walked out of her house and never came back. In that time, the police had many red herrings; possible sightings, people claiming to know Vivienne, and even some demented souls that said they had killed her. All turned out to be false.

In the first weeks of her disappearance, all I wanted to do was drink, sleep, repeat. After I recovered from my initial inebriated slumber some weeks later, I decided it was time that I tried to help.

---

1. *https://en.wikipedia.org/wiki/Mary_Elizabeth_Frye*

During that first year, I moved into Viv's house and gave up my own - just in case she did return. I joined search parties, made door-to-door enquiries, and held vigils in her honour. The outpouring of love and support was monumental. There were times I genuinely felt hopeful. Then there were days I just didn't want to get out of bed. In all honesty, I had more bad days than good.

My father tried to reach out to me several times, not to answer my burning questions but to beg for my attention. I just dodged his phone calls and knocks at the door. At times, I saw him lurking in the distance within my peripheral vision. I'd be out on a jog and I'd catch him sitting on a park bench at the top of the hill, or I'd be on my way home from work and I'd see him sheltered in a bus stop across the street. Once, he called after me, once I saw him wave. Neither time did I respond.

Then the letters started, messages of love and sorrow. I couldn't bring myself to keep opening them week after week, and eventually, they too stopped. I shopped at different supermarkets, hung out in different neighbourhoods, avoided anywhere that linked me back to him, but it was no good. The saying out of sight, out of mind is bullshit. I thought about him every time I closed my eyes before I slept, and then every morning when I woke, alongside Grace and Vivienne. He seeped his way into my thoughts like a virus, like a poison, tainting and infecting the beauty of those I held dear. The anger and resentment inside me were toxic.

I knew I could not keep holding onto the past. The proximity to him and living in Viv's home were daily reminders of my torment. He'd never leave Haxby, but I could. As hard as it was to leave Viv's house, I knew that my only chance at happiness was to finally take my mother's advice on board:

As my dying wish, please obey this instruction. Rid yourself of him and start a new life.

So that's what I did.

Part two

Second chances

19

Zoe

Stepping off the plane, I stood tall with newfound self-assurance. My eyes gleamed wishfully as I motioned into the light, letting go of the darkness that once shrouded me. Could this place really be one of the happiest on the planet? Copenhagen wasn't top of my list but that's what made it so perfect. No one would think to look for me here.

For the first time in a long time, I felt a spring in my step. Upon boarding the train to the city centre, I was caught off guard. In the carriage window's reflection, there was a girl with an unfamiliar smile stretched across her face. After a moment, I realised the girl was me. The chuckle that proceeded was equally as foreign. Passengers gawked, making me giggle even more. Shredding my life in Haxby wasn't a clean break by any means. If someone looked closely enough, they'd see a slight hesitation etched into my iris, but I would work hard on keeping that hidden.

My studio apartment was located a hop, skip and a jump away from the train station in the Meatpacking District – apparently one of the coolest spots to reside. The space was newly renovated whilst still conserving its original Danish charm. White walls echoed the neutral, soft furnishings. The only colour in the room emanated from a large canvas of the city that hung above the tiny sofa.

After unpacking and buying some basic groceries from the closet shop, I attempted to relax in front of the TV. I tossed and turned on the compact couch, flicking aimlessly from channel to channel.

Adrenaline coursed through my veins as the city summoned me from afar. I ached to get back out and explore. As twilight descended across the metropolis, my feet hit the curb.

Like a bee gravitates to pollen, I followed the twinkling lights and soft jazz music beyond the station. Tivoli Gardens sparkled against the navy sky. My mouth fell open the closer I inspected its grandeur. As I made my way through the imposing archway, the true scale of its festivities flooded my senses. Sweeping rollercoasters adorned the air, strung lanterns and multi-coloured illuminations shone like beaming confetti.

Strolling along the path my nose picked up the sweet smell of pastries and chocolate. I gave in to my temptations and purchased a sugary doughnut. Underneath a weeping willow, I rested on a metal bench that was nestled next to the lake and towering Chinese pagoda. The first bite transported me back to my childhood. I closed my eyes and saw myself sat along the British shorefront, enjoying the delicacies of a seaside kiosk.

As I opened my eyes, I noticed a man mirroring me opposite the water. Was he looking at me too?

I turned around to see if anyone was stood behind me. No one. Still, he held his gaze. If it wasn't for the depths of the evening light, he'd be able to see the crimson flush against my cheeks. Before I could wallow in my embarrassment further, he waved in my direction. I found myself waving back. My hand was a little closer to my body than his. He stood up and started walking away from the bench he once sat on. I thought he'd grown bored of our simple exchanges, but I noticed him begin to move towards me. I panicked. Should I stand and shake his hand?

I opted for budging up to one side, making room for him to sit next to me. There was a sudden light breeze that sent strands of hair across my face. I self-consciously pushed them aside as he approached.

Out came a gravely Danish accent, "Hej, må jeg sidde?" Thick, straight eyebrows hooded his grey-blue eyes that were fixed onto mine. His own shoulder-length, tawny locks flowed gently in the wind. He tucked one side behind his ear as he gestured to the bench I was sat on.

Unquestionably, now he could make out my reddened complexion, "Sorry, English?"

"May I sit?"

"Yes, of course." I patted my hand against the metal, emphasising my point. "You speak English then?"

"Yes, most Danish do. We find tourists do not learn the Danish language as freely."

Now he was closer, I could better inspect his face. I noticed his forehead bore several distinguished, fine wrinkles. I wondered how old he was. Stubble framed his full mouth. Above, he had a robust, strong nose. A manly nose.

I raised my hand, "Guilty as charged."

"What is your name, English girl?"

As he turned his head to face me more fully, I saw a deep-set dimple in the centre of his chin. I followed the nape of his neck and watched as his pronounced Adam's apple bounced as he swallowed.

I hesitated, this was my time to be anyone, anyone at all. I found myself struggling to come up with an interesting name, so I just settled on the one I already had. "My name is Zoe, and yours?"

"Jesper. It is a pleasure to meet you, Zoe." He stretched out his hand in what felt like a tongue-in-cheek formality.

I slowly slid my palm against his and shook. "It is lovely to meet you too," I smiled.

"So, Zoe, what are you doing here in Copenhagen? Besides enjoying a doughnut."

I felt his body shuffle a tad closer to mine. I decided I could be honest without needing to divulge too many depressing details.

"I've actually just moved here. This is my first day in Copenhagen."

"What enticed you to move to Denmark?"

His eyes looked glossy with the warm ambience that surrounded us. He didn't blink for even a second when he spoke to me. I smoothed my cascading hair between my fingers.

"I needed to make a change. Denmark just so happens to be one of the happiest places to live."

He made a long sigh before he replied, "Happiness is what you make it. You don't find it," he says, searching the stars, "unless you happen to be sat opposite a beautiful stranger in Tivoli Gardens. Can I ask, are you alone in Copenhagen?"

I was taken aback by his forwardness but also a little impressed too.

"Yes," I breathed.

"Then I must tell you something else."

The seriousness in his voice worried me. Was this the part where he confessed a horrible ailment or revealed he had a wife?

"What is it?"

"You have sugar... on your chin."

"Oh god, do I?" I began frantically wiping around my mouth with my hands. No wonder he's been staring at me so intently.

"Here, let me."

His thumb delicately rubbed the skin beneath my bottom lip, pulling my mouth slightly open. My breath accelerated. I hadn't felt a man's touch for so long. As my eyes fluttered from his hand to his silver eyes once more, I could feel the electricity pulling me to him like a magnet. No longer thinking, but falling, I closed the space between us with a kiss. A soft, sensual kiss. From then on, I was spellbound.

20

Grace - Before

Dear diary,
      He's doing it again.

21

Zoe

Jesper and I moved in together after a month of dating. We were virtually inseparable, except when I was working at the coffee shop and he was at the office.

Jesper worked as an architect. One of my favourite things to do with him was to saunter around the city admiring buildings and listening to him pour over every intimate detail. Each curve or line had a specific purpose I never knew. The way he spoke about design was like a poet rejoicing their muse.

He was like no man that I'd ever met. With Jesper, I could be myself. Well, my new and improved self. He knew my mother had died of cancer some time ago and that I didn't like to talk about it. When the subject of the father arose, I simply said we'd lost touch - which we had. He just didn't know I was the reason we stayed apart. I didn't even know where to begin with Vivienne.

Then I got the news, and all I wanted to do was call Viv up and tell her, "I'm pregnant!"

"What?" Jesper gasped, almost dropping his coffee cup. He settled it down on the kitchen countertop and looked at me startled.

"I said, I'm pregnant!" I was practically jumping around with glee. Jesper and I had been trying unsuccessfully for a couple of months. Even though we hadn't been together for very long, age wasn't on our side, and we were madly and insanely in love.

Jesper staggered towards me, arms open wide, "That's wonderful," he proclaimed as his arms embraced my body, "are you sure?"

"Yes, very sure. We're going to have a baby." I dangled the pregnancy test in front of him for proof. "Look, two lines. That means it's positive. Also, I've missed my period. I didn't want to say anything too soon, so I waited until I took the test. Ta-da!"

Jesper squeezed me tight and whispered, "We're going to have a baby."

We stayed like that, cocooned in blissful wonderment, for some time. Simply swaying together to a silent song only we could hear. Then, out of nowhere, tears descended. Suddenly, I felt overwhelmed with sadness. Before more tears could fall, I retracted backwards from Jesper and sheltered myself in the bathroom.

"Is everything okay?"

The concern in Jesper's voice made me cry even harder.

"I...I... just need a minute." I sat, crumpled over my knees on the toilet seat. In this sheer moment of joy, I was paralysed by grief. This was something I envisioned telling my mother about. I imagined her beautiful face beaming with delight. It would have been her arms cradling me. I didn't even have my best friend here to confide in or a father. I had no one.

"Let me in, Zoe, I want to help."

I sat up and stared at myself in the mirror, fixing my makeup and flattening my clothes. I'd seen that look in my eyes before on the day that I went to the police station with Viv to incriminate my father. Conviction. I knew it was time. Now or never. I just hoped Jesper could handle the truth. All of it.

I emerged from the bathroom and hugged him longingly. It gave me a brief moment of respite. I could just forgo the trouble and blame my mood swing on early pregnancy hormones. What if Jesper looked at me differently after he knew the same killer blood of my father flowed through my veins? Blood that would be passed on to our child. Would he want to take on such a burden? There was only one way to find out.

"Jesper, we need to talk," I said as we transitioned to the couch. I took both his firm hands in mine, and began, fixed on the floor as I spoke, "There are some things...things about my life I think you should know. There is a reason I'm so closed off when it comes to talking about my father."

"You can tell me anything, Zoe. You know that."

Still averting direct eye contact, I continued, reassured by Jesper's gentle squeeze. "I'm afraid, when I tell you, you won't want me anymore."

Jesper clutched my hands tighter, forcing me to look him in the eye, "I will always want you."

I truly believed him. Jesper was the kindest soul I'd ever known. The past months had been the best of my entire life. How could I expect this man to allow me to carry his child, when I haven't even allowed him to hear my entire story? I owe him everything, and nothing I do can ever repay what he has given me, a new beginning. The least I can do is be sincere.

The words blurted out, "My father... he's a murderer." Seconds passed without either of us speaking. This was something nobody knew how to talk about. Nobody prepared for such a conversation. Nobody expects such a conversation to even occur.

"Is he in jail?" Jesper finally responded.

"No, he isn't. He was never even prosecuted for the murders. You see, what I should have said was I think my father is a murderer."

"Wait...I'm confused, what would make you think that?"

"My mother. She left me a letter saying as much... before she died. I still have it if you'd like to take a look?"

Upon Jesper nodding his head, I collected the letter from my jewellery box. I kept it tucked neatly under an internal tray. Safe. My hand trembled as I gave it to him. I sat and watched as his eyes scanned left to right along the page. I had to keep my palms against my thighs to stop them from shaking. After reading the letter, he passed it back to me without a single comment.

"So?"

"Your mother gave you this letter?"

"...Not exactly, I found it. She'd left it in a jacket she'd promised I could have when she died." Jesper's face made me feel like I was insane. "Listen, I know my mother's handwriting okay? This is her, and why would she lie about such things? Then there are the cases that we found."

"We?"

"I had a best friend back then, called Vivienne. She helped me research unsolved murders – to see if any fit. There were women who lived near where I lived. Women that died on the same nights my father was unaccounted for."

Jesper frowned. Was it in confusion or disappointment?

"Where is Vivienne now?"

"That's another thing. She went missing after we went to the police with everything we'd discovered...Stop looking at me like that!"

"I'm not! This is an awful lot to take in."

I stood up, pacing the room defiantly.

"You don't know, Jesper. You don't understand. My best friend went missing just after the police questioned my father! What does that tell you?"

"I don't know. Your right, I don't know. A moment ago I was the happiest guy on the planet. Now, I'm just finding out about all this." Jesper was hunched over, rubbing his temples profusely.

I grabbed my handbag and house keys and angled for the front door. "Well, why don't I give you some time to think." With that, I marched out onto the street, my face wet with tears.

The sky was uncharacteristically grey overhead. I had no destination in mind. I just kept moving forward. Away. How must have all that sounded to someone on the outside? For so long, this was my secret to keep. All that kept me from sharing my past was the hurt it could cause. I never even considered whether Jesper would believe me. Now it's out in the open, it cannot be undone. I was stupid to not tell Jesper all this before I was pregnant. How could I be so inconsiderate?

My breathing steadied and my walk slowed to a stop. I can't allow my father to come between us. Whether Jesper understands or not, he makes me happy. That's all I want. To be happy. Resolved, I turned back home with my tail between my legs. At the bottom of the street, I could see Jesper wandering about. He came after me. I stroked my belly. He came after us.

"Sorry. I didn't mean to storm out like that."

"Come here," Jesper said as he nuzzled my hair with kisses. "Why didn't you ever say anything?"

"I guess I wasn't ready. Moving here was my escape. That's why I came. Then I met you, and I've been swept up in...well in you! I didn't want to push you away."

Jesper's fingers threaded through mine, "Let's go back inside, and this time, start from the top."

22

Zoe

8 months later

It was summer and the heat was unbearable. I hadn't slept properly for weeks, and Jesper now had to help me get dressed. I'd just about managed to keep working on my feet, serving countless Laddes (Danish for Lattes) at Original Kaffe, but today was my last shift.

Original Kaffe had a cool, hipster vibe only the Danish could authentically pull off. People came here to relax. To connect with their friends. It was a simple job, but it was also a fun job. I'd mastered embellishing foam with flowers and hearts, and I'd made my own friends here too.

I wiped the sweat from my brow as I called up the last order of the day over the sound of instrumental music.

Henrik clapped behind me as the customer came to collect her drink, "Congratulations, Zoe, your last cup of coffee."

I could only see half of his face between the bulbous lights that dangled at differing heights across the ceiling, looking like an art installation.

Henrik owned the coffee shop and thankfully was as fluent as Jesper when it came to speaking my mother tongue. Sometimes, I wanted to converse with him in Danish, to test myself, but Henrik always spoke to me in English. Maybe he thought I was no good. If so, he'd probably be right.

"So, do you have exciting plans for tonight?" Henrik asked, hand on hip, bushy brow arched. I suspected he was gay when we first met but then he'd revealed he had a wife and three children on a staff night out. I guess I'd misplaced his bouncy, carefree persona – still, chatting with him felt like talking with one of the girls.

"Oh yeah, a bottle of wine, night on the town, you know, the usual."

"Just because you're pregnant doesn't mean you can't have fun, girl. You should make the most of this time. You'll be wishing you had it back when the baby comes. Don't tell me I didn't warn you!"

"You really are the best boss. Did you know that?"

Henrik took a bow, dodging the tea towel that I'd launched at him. "I did actually."

The towel missed him by a mile and landed between a couple of rickety, unvarnished coffee tables. He launched it back at me with a grin and told me to get on my way. I sucked in a satisfying breath and stared at the matte white walls with pockets of brickwork showing through. I was going to miss coming to work, but I was also eager to start this next phase in my life.

When I finally got home, the sweat had soaked through my vest. Jesper wasn't due to be home until later, so I decided to take a cool shower. Something I enjoyed doing when Jesper wasn't around was watching English television. Sometimes I missed England, and this was my way of staying in touch.

My favourite thing to watch was British morning talk shows. Danish news didn't have the same flair as This Morning or Loose Women. Jesper didn't get the appeal of such programmes, but to me, they were like comfort food.

I positioned my laptop on my bed as I undressed and hit play. The show was today's date but had aired hours previously. I zoned out at the theme tune and overview of headlines until I heard a name that I instantly recognised. I turned the volume up to a hundred and listened intently.

Breaking news, the body of Vivienne Cooper has been found at North York Moors National Park. Ellaine Johnson has the latest.

My blood ran cold; my throat closed shut. I tried to listen intently over the thump of my heart.

Ellaine: Thanks, Audrey. The 28-year-old newspaper journalist was reported missing on 6th March 2015 after leaving her home in York around 9:30 am, never to be seen again. Although many had held out hope for Vivienne's safe return, Vivienne's family chose to declare her dead in 2022 following years of no leads. Today, the family finally have some closure on what happened to their daughter on that fateful morning. I'm joined with DC Wilde for the latest on this discovery. DC Wilde, what can you tell us about the nature of Vivienne's death?

DC Wilde: At this time, we can reveal Vivienne died of suspected stab wounds. A more comprehensive autopsy report will confirm this in due course.

Ellaine: What can you tell us about where and how Vivienne's body was found?

DC Wilde: I cannot say too much about the circumstances of her discovery, but what I can detail is that Vivienne's remains were identified by two men camping on the Northern Moors.

Ellaine: Do you have any suspects in custody for the murder?

DC Wilde: As this is now an open homicide inquiry, we cannot comment on any current suspects.

Ellaine: Thank you, DC Wilde. The family has asked for people to respect their privacy at this time. Back to you, Audrey.

I must have rewound and replayed the segment a dozen times. Pictures of Viv, my Viv, filled the screen. Her fiery hair, her angled face, frozen in time. It was official. Vivienne was dead.

I could feel my body begin to hyperventilate. I couldn't breathe. Even at her funeral, I didn't believe she was actually dead. And the way she died. Stabbed. I had pretended that she'd moved abroad like me and started again. Deep down, something dark gnawed away at me. I'd suppressed that thought deep within me, worrying that acknowledging it would somehow make it true. My worst fears had materialised. My best friend was murdered, and I knew exactly who did it.

I was on all fours now, panting. A wave of pain pulsated through my back and lower abdomen. I scrambled for my mobile, moaning as I fought for breath. A scream escaped my lips. As my eyes blurred and my water broke, I managed to find his name in my contacts.

"...Jesper...Jesper...agh, I think I'm going into labour."

23

Zoe

By the time we arrived at the hospital, the pain had worsened. I could hear other women howling through their pain in the adjoining rooms. Jesper looked concerned as he spoke to the midwife.

"She isn't due for another month, what's going on?"

He spoke English for my benefit. We'd chosen an English-speaking hospital so that I could understand what was going on.

"Sometimes women can go into early labour, it is rare, but it happens. She is in safe hands."

A searing pain pulsated through my cervix. I let out a primal groan and had a sudden urge to push. Jesper's hand held mine firmly as he consoled me.

"I'm here, I'm here. Everything is going to be alright."

"Her contractions are every three minutes." A hand reached inside me. "Best wheel her into the delivery room."

My body was ripping apart, I was sure of it. My skin tensed with a blistering heat. I couldn't believe my mother went through this on her own.

"Zoe, we are going to give you some gas and air for the pain, but we don't have time for an epidural. Your baby is on its way now."

A mask was placed across my mouth, and I began to suck in the medicated air. Again. Again. Again. My mind fogged and my body softened, just a little. I don't know how long I zoned in and out of pain and lucidity for. All sense of time blended into one moment of torment. A midwife finally came to my aid.

"Zoe, you're going to have to start pushing, okay? On the next contraction, I want you to push down."

My legs were spread eagle in stirrups, and I wondered where Jesper was stood.

I grunted his name through gritted teeth, "Jesper?"

He spoke from the left side of my head, "I'm here, you can do this."

Lightning rods tore through me once more, and I pushed hard. Waves of nausea and aching consumed my body.

"I can't...do this. I'm not strong enough," I sobbed.

"Yes, you are. You have overcome so much in your life, you can do this. Do this for Grace. Do this for me. Do this for our baby, Zoe."

Another contraction raged inside of me. I gripped the sides of the bed and pushed harder this time. I kept pushing, not breathing, not thinking, just pushing.

"That's it, Zoe, I can see the head. One more push."

"You are doing so great."

I was exhausted. I didn't know how to muster any more strength. When the next contraction struck, I willed every last ounce of energy that I had and pushed. A carousel of people came into vision, my mother, Vivienne, my father. Anger and frustration flooded through me, helping me to keep on fighting.

Then I felt it, my baby leaving me. Searing heat morphed into exhilaration. People rushed around in a blur, talking fast. "It's a baby girl! Congratulations."

A baby girl. My baby girl. I could hear her tiny, piercing cries in the distance. I couldn't keep my eyes open. I was slipping away. Beeping, such loud beeping.

As I let my body sink away, I heard them shouting over and over, "She's haemorrhaging!"

24

Zoe

My mother caressed my cheek lovingly. Soft, pearlescent light danced around her. Golden tresses feathered across her face as if she were caught mid-breeze, but I could feel no wind. Her eyes glistened bright as she smiled. White teeth sandwiched between scarlet lips. She was soundlessly talking, mouthing something I couldn't make out. I stretched out to touch her, but I could not reach. My body locked without motion. Her features began to fade and dispel into the light until there was no trace of her left; only specks of dust floating in cloud and the rhythmic beep of machines.

"I thought you'd died." I heard, as my eyes fluttered open.

The first thing that I noticed was the white bed that I laid on and the needle and tube inserted in my hand. Then, there by my side, Jesper emerged.

"Jesper? Where am I?" I croaked, as Jesper flung his arms around my chest.

"You are in the hospital still. You gave us quite a scare. How do you feel?"

We? Who else is there? Everything is muddled in my mind, am I missing something?

"What happened?"

"You lost a lot of blood after giving birth. You had to have a blood transfusion... we didn't know if you'd make it."

I immediately clasped my stomach. I had my baby! The memory rushed back to me. A girl they said. Her cries like an echo in a well.

"Is she okay?" I panicked.

"She's sleeping, next to you in her crib. Would you like to hold her? Do you feel ready?"

"Yes, bring her to me, please."

He cradled our daughter in his arms. She was wrapped snug in a blanket and hat with just her rosy face poking out, eyes still shut.

"Isn't she beautiful, just like her mum?"

She was so tiny and light in my arms. A precious, beautiful bundle indeed. I watched her as she breathed small breaths, safe in the crook of my arm. It was as if every cell in my being radiated with love. The energy was so strong I swear you could see it bouncing between us in all its shimmering glory. I placed a kiss on her forehead and wondered what to name her.

"Clara. She looks like a Clara, don't you think?"

"Sounds perfect," Jesper agreed.

When I was finally given the all clear and discharged from hospital some days later, the protected bubble that I felt dissipated. We were on our own. In the big wide world. The notion was terrifying. Jesper took immediate control of us both. He drove incessantly slow all the way home to the sheer annoyance of everyone else on the road, constantly checking in with how I felt. How did I feel?

Having a baby was like nothing else I'd ever experienced. It is an indescribable act. One of those life experiences you can only understand when you experience it for yourself. I was overjoyed and thrilled, but I was also afraid and anxious. Weirdly, I'd never felt closer to my mother. I now knew exactly why she was a worrier. Why she watched over me so much. The thought of ever taking my eyes off Clara and her getting hurt was heart-wrenching. I just wish my mother was still here for me to tell her as much.

"You've had a lot of calls from your family back in England - Aunt Caitlyn and Darcey, Vivienne's parents, Tracy and Phil. We should send them a little video when we get home."

Vivienne. I'd completely forgotten about Viv's body being found.

"Did you speak to Tracy or Phil?"

"Yes, I had a phone call with Tracy. Your Aunt told them when you went into early labour...and when you...well...you know. They wanted to know if you were okay."

"Did they mention anything about Viv?"

"I didn't want to tell you yet, in case you weren't ready. They found Vivienne's body, Zoe. I'm sorry."

Flashbacks of me listening to the news report played out in my head. I could see myself struggling on the floor, writhing in pain as the contractions began.

"Actually, I already know. The day I went into labour was the day that I found out. I was listening to the news, and I guess the shock of it all brought on the labour."

Jesper sighed, "Zoe, I...I'm just so sorry. I should have been there more. You shouldn't have been working such long hours at the coffee shop. All this stress, it was never going to be good for you and Clara."

"It's all ancient history. I've got my own family to look after now," I said, "We should show Clara off. A video sounds like a great idea."

I tried to sound as genuine as possible. Deep down, another emotion loomed. A hatred I'd left to languish was resurrecting. Untamed and underfed. Intertwined within this resentment a new feeling was ablaze. Something primitive, protective. I felt no fear. Just a desire to put all the wrongs right. For I would not bring my daughter up in a world where her murderous Grandfather could lay a single finger upon her head.

25

Zoe

Haxby was as if I'd never left. It had taken Jesper some convincing, but he wanted to see where I had come from. Besides, Aunt Caitlyn and Darcey were desperate to meet Clara. As were Vivienne's parents.

Jesper had never been to England at all. I felt a little ashamed as we drove through the boxy council estates and dreary parks, practically prehistoric compared to the fashionable beauty of Copenhagen.

"York city centre is lovely. Just you wait and see."

As if reading my mind he replied, "That would be great. Haxby seems nice though, quaint."

"There are some nice parts. I'll have to give you and Clara the grand tour," I caught sight of a playground I used to hang out in as a kid, "Look over, that was where I had my very first kiss. Jealous?"

"Of the kiss or the location?"

"Very funny. England is a great place to grow up. Not everything is picture-postcard but it's home."

"It was home. Now you have a new home, with us. Doesn't she Clara?"

I was glad to not live in Haxby anymore - or England for that matter - but I couldn't shake the feeling of comfort these drabbed streets gave me. In spite of all the tragedy that had happened here, I still had many fond memories.

The car satnav had informed us that we'd arrived at our destination. It had been so long that I'd totally forgotten the route. We parked up just as Clara began to stir.

"So which house is your aunt's?"

"That one there, with the dove grey door."

"Dove grey? I think my architectural influence is rubbing off on you."

"No, I remember. That was the paint name. Dove grey. Darcey and I painted it for her. Not a bad job aye?"

Jesper looked the door up and down like he was eyeing up a woman. "Not bad at all. I'll have to get you doing our house up, now I know I can trust you with a paintbrush."

A wry smirk spread across my face. I couldn't hold it in place for long. Aunt Caitlyn didn't live far from my childhood home. I wondered if my father still lived there.

"Let's head in, Clara's getting hungry."

Aunt Caitlyn practically smothered me as soon as I made it through the door. She briefly greeted Jesper before proceeding to coo over Clara, announcing how wonderful she was.

"Doesn't she look like you, Zoe? Gosh, it is like seeing double."

"Absolutely!" Jesper interjected.

"Where's Darcey? I'd love to see her," I said, eager to get the focus away from myself.

"She'll be here soon. She said she'd come straight from work. We've all been so excited."

Wrinkles surrounded her eyes as she grinned. Caitlyn had aged so much since I last saw her. She'd had her hair cut short, and I could see sprouts of silver hair that turned almost translucent in the afternoon sun.

"You've brought the weather back with you."

"Don't worry, we get rain in Denmark too," Jesper replied.

We digressed to chitchat about Danish life and how we were finding parenthood.

"It isn't easy, but it's the greatest gift. And you two. You make the most stunning couple, you really do. I'm so happy for you both."

Caitlyn broke down then. Unable to restrain the flood of emotion flooding from every pore.

"I'm so sorry, I just can't help thinking about Grace and how proud she'd be."

I sniffled back a tear of my own, attempting to squash the image of my own mother embracing my daughter. After feeding Clara, we spent hours leading up to Darcey's arrival looking over baby pictures and of course, Aunt Caitlyn held her the entire time.

When Darcey arrived, we reminisced about the old days. She too fell head over heels for Clara and insisted she be the one to put her down for a nap. Jesper and Aunt Caitlyn were busy preparing dinner for us all, so as Darcey came out of the bedroom, I took the opportunity to take her aside for a quiet word.

"Darcey, can I ask you to do something for me?"

"Of course, anything, what's the matter?"

"This has to stay between us. You can't say anything to Aunt Caitlyn or Jesper, okay?"

"...Okay, but you're scaring me, Zoe. What's going on?"

I lowered my voice, whispering now, "I need you to call me tomorrow morning, pretending you've bumped into an old friend, and you want us all to catch up over lunch."

"...Why?"

"So I have a reason to leave the house, without Clara or Jesper."

"So you don't actually want to go out for lunch?"

"No...I...I want to go and see my dad."

Darcey didn't say anything, just stared blankly. Nobody knew why we'd fallen out. I didn't know if he'd told them the truth or made up some fictitious story.

"Are we never going to talk about why the police questioned him over Vivienne's death?"

I felt queasy, what happened after I left?

"What? The police interviewed him?"

"Yeah, I figured that's why you hadn't told him about Clara yet?"

"So he didn't go to jail?"

"No, the police came and spoke to us too, asked about his character. His past. It was so strange. I thought they'd reach out to you too. Did they not?"

"No...not that I can recall. Do you guys think he had anything to do with Viv's disappearance?" I was fishing here, gaging the reaction.

"Me? No. Never. My mum, however, was a little less unconvinced. Still has her doubts I think."

"Does he still live in the same house?"

"Yeah, never moved. Even after all the suspicion. He's a bit of a recluse now. Mum thinks he has a drinking problem. I don't know if it is safe for you to visit him on your own, Zoe. Let me come."

I considered her offer briefly. My plan had no way of working if she was there, "I need to go alone, Darcey. I need to ask him myself, once and for all. So do I have your help?"

Darcey bit her lip and huffed.

"What time should I call?"

26
Zoe

The next day, Jesper bought the excuse hook, line, and sinker. I knew if Darcey rang at eleven am Clara would be having one of her mid-morning naps, so I would have a reason not to take her with me.

"I'll take him into town later if you like? Show him and Clara the best York has to offer? You could meet up with us when you're done," Caitlyn offered.

Jesper's eyes shone with delight, "I would like to get out of the house, see the sights."

"Sounds like a plan. You guys go ahead without me, and I'll just call you when I'm done."

Guilt rose from my gut, making my throat dry and metallic tasting. This was the first outright deceitful thing that I'd done in my relationship with Jesper. Everything else was an avoidance of the truth but this was a pure lie.

I kissed both him and Clara tenderly, trying my best not to cry. I was deceiving her too, abandoning her for selfish reasons. Reasons that I had to remember were valid and righteous.

"I love you," I murmured as I left the house, focused on the task in hand.

My house was a dishevelled shell of its former self. Plants were overgrown, paint was chipping, and the curtains were shut. My once happy family home now felt so uninviting. The key rolled over in my fingers. I debated whether to knock, but I didn't want to risk him closing the door in my face. Letting myself in was the only sure-fire way of guaranteeing an entrance.

The jagged metal slid into the lock and turned. I paused momentarily before proceeding inside. The air was pungent with liquor. Post piled up behind the door as if nobody had lived here for years. I wandered into the lounge and searched around for any sign of life. Empty glass bottles littered the floor. The bin in the kitchen was overflowing with rubbish. Pots, crusted with the remnants of takeout grease, stacked high in the sink. What had this place become?

I made my way up the stairs, glancing at the dusty photographs of my mother hung on the wall. She was so house proud when she was alive. She'd be turning in her grave if she could see the dire disrepair of her home.

I poked my head into the stale bathroom, then my untouched bedroom. No one. The last room was their bedroom.

"Dad?" I called as I entered, the word devoid of sentiment.

There, surrounded by scrupled, dirty sheets sat my father. Or a shadow of my father. Overweight, bearded, and sallow he looked like a complete stranger.

He turned his head to face me, with a glass look in his eye.

"Zoe? Is that you?" he croaked.

"We need to talk."

Like a retired ex-boxer, he looked defeated. His head hung in shame. He pulled a packet of cigarettes from his pocket and struck a match. He lost himself in the glow of the flame for a moment, before igniting his cigarette and taking a deep inhale.

"Ask me anything."

I wasn't expecting him to be so open. Looking at this pathetic man in front of me, it was hard to imagine him capable of killing someone. I inched closer, as close as I could stand, making sure I spoke as clear as possible.

"I need to know; did you murder Vivienne?"

He took another long drag and blew the smoke away from me. "I heard you had a baby."

How on earth did he know that? Had Aunt Caitlyn told him? Darcey?

"Don't avoid the question. Did you kill Vivienne?" My voice an octave higher now.

"Can I meet her?"

"Dad, I'm not playing this game with you. You said I could ask you anything, so let's talk."

"I want to see her before...before I confess."

Even though I knew he was guilty, the impending conversation filled me with dread. I knew I had to stay strong, but the rage was building inside of me.

"Confess to what?"

"I did it. I killed Vivienne."

This was good. He'd spoken so matter of fact. The police couldn't discredit this proof.

"Why? Why did you kill her?"

He closed his eyes and mumbled under his breath.

"Speak up!" I stood tall over him now, my chest heaving with adrenalin.

"You've grown up to be so beautiful, Zoe. Just like your mother. I bet your daughter is just as lovely."

"You don't get to talk about her. Either of them, not after what you've done. I'm only going to ask you this one more time, and then I'm going to leave and I'm never going to come back. Why?"

He covered his face with his hands, and for a second, I thought he was about to cry.

"She was ruining everything. She was coming between us...when the police interrogated me about those murders, I was so shocked. I asked where they had gotten such a stupid idea, and they said they'd had an anonymous letter, incriminating me."

So the police didn't tell him it was me who passed on the letter.

"I'd been to your house, to see if you knew anything about it. When you weren't in, I went to the only other place I thought you could be. That's when I saw her."

I imagined Viv setting her eyes on him as she left her house, just metres away from me. How different this day would have played out if I had only gone with her!

"I asked her what was going on and she started shouting about the murders. I didn't want anyone to hear, so I asked her to sit in my car so we could talk. Just talk. I never intended to...to..."

My fists clenched. For the first time in my life, I actually felt like I wanted to hurt someone. I wanted to hurt my father.

"And then what happened?"

"We drove, I don't know where, I just wanted to find somewhere quiet, secluded, where we wouldn't be interrupted. Vivienne was so angry. I'd never seen her like that. She kept telling me I'd never see you again – that I'd die alone. My whole world was falling apart. I just wanted her to stop. That's when I struck her."

This can't be the full story.

"The police said she died of knife wounds."

"She came around and wanted to get out of the car. She kept screaming and shaking the car handle, but I couldn't let her leave in that state. I knew she'd run straight back to you or the police and make me look even worse! I...I...had my tools in the back. All the talk of killing with the police earlier, kept going round in my head. I caught sight of a silver hacksaw. That's when the idea popped into my head...and...when things got ugly."

I saw an empty spirit bottle on the side, and an unwelcomed thought crossed my mind. I could strike him. Old and decrepit as he is now. He'd be easy pickings.

I shook my head profusely. No. I would never stoop to his level. I am nothing like this man.

"Did you murder those other women?"

"No, Zoe, I swear on your mother's grave I had never killed before then."

"Why would you kill Viv if you had nothing to hide? I don't believe you!"

His cigarette was burnt down to the stub, but he continued to hold it. "I guess I wouldn't believe me either. I really am sorry, Zoe."

"I'm not. This time, you are going to get what you deserve."

I turned on my heel abruptly and bounded down the stairs, scared that he'd chase after me. As soon as I made it outside to my car, I locked the doors. Pulling out my phone I hit STOP, then dialled 999.

"Police...my father just confessed to a murder and I have recorded every word of it."

27

Grace – Before

Dear diary,

As I am slowly dying, James is having an affair. The affair itself, I may have been able to grapple with. We haven't been having sex since I started treatment so that I might have understood, but what I cannot tolerate is who he is having an affair with.

Discovering the sordid texts messages between them made me physically sick. Sicker than I am now. The one person he chooses out of every other possible whore, is Vivienne. I have so many unanswered questions screaming at me. When did it start? How old was she when this began? What about Zoe – did he think of her feelings during any of this? God, the smut they wrote to one another! And then there was the message signed, I love you. What an absolute joke.

Beyond the betrayal, the hurt, I am angry. Unbelievably angry. After all the shit that I have put up with over the years, he falls in love with his daughter's best friend. The fucking nerve. All my life James has gotten away with murder. He even missed Zoe's birth. Was he having an affair with me back then too? I feel so bloody stupid.

The hardest part is knowing that when I die, all of this will be out of my control. He won't need to answer for any of it. Zoe will keep thinking her father is the apple of her eye, and Vivienne will come to my funeral before continuing her disgusting antics.

Confronting James won't end the affair. I can't exactly spend my remaining days spying on him. And I can't tell my darling Zoe the truth. I won't ruin her friendship. If she doesn't believe me, she'd hate me. Her last memory of me would be tainted forever. Zoe just needs to rid herself of them. Start anew. But what could I possibly say to get her to do that?

28

Zoe

Now

Crows squawk overhead. The air feels mild for winter, but I am still wrapped up in my floor-length, woollen coat. Dawn is breaking and the sky is streaked with pastel pinks and blues. I lay the bouquet of lilies on her grave – her favourite.

"Are we going to head to Vivienne's grave next, mum?" Clara asks.

"After, I just want to stay here a while longer."

We holiday back and forth between Denmark and England since my father's arrest. I never did go visit him.

My mobile rings in my pocket, and at first, I assume it is James. I take it out, and my brows furrow when I see who is calling.

"Aunt Caitlyn, how are you?"

A long pause ensues.

"You better come over, Zoe. I've found something that you're going to want to see."

"Is everything, okay?" I wonder if she is confused like my mother was when she was having chemo.

"It's about Grace. When you asked me to sell your mum and dad's house," the way she says dad sounds odd on her tongue - forced. "Well, I took some things that I thought you'd want to keep or pass down to dear Clara. I've only just gotten around to looking through it myself. That's when I found it."

Clara tugs on my arm, telling me she is cold and bored and wants to leave. Her voice is white noise, distant and faded to the crashing worry in my chest.

"Found what?" My breath a flume of white in the cold air. My eyes transfix onto Grace's headstone.

Devoted Mother, loved by all who knew her.

"A diary," she said soberly. "It's time to tell you the truth. Can you come over?"

I sway a little and find myself gripping Clara's shoulder to stay afloat. Clara mutters concern, but I ignore her – unable to do anything else but strain, "The truth about what?"

"About everything, Zoe."

I glance at my watch and register how soon we need to meet James for our return flight home. I find the plane tickets in my bag, take them out, and tear them up.

"I'm on my way."

I cancel the call and turn to Clara; her face a beacon of purity and innocence.

"Looks like we're going to stay here a while longer, darling."

"Why?" she whines, her expression taut.

I search the sky and then turn to her. "I have unfinished business."

29

Grace Before

Dear diary,

As I lay in bed, riddled with an incurable cancer, I weigh up the value of my life. The choices that I had made. I thought I knew myself once upon a time, but until you have been pushed to the brink of death, you will never understand how that will truly impact you. I was a person without fear, a person capable of anything. Crossing me again, well, you'd only have yourself to blame.

I deserve to die; I know that. I have done horrible things, but what I am not guilty of is being a bad mother. I always put Zoe first. You have to understand, writing that letter was extremely difficult for me. Everything I did was to protect Zoe. James being in a relationship with Vivienne, after everything I had done for our family, was the tipping point.

I have nothing to lose.

In death, I can rewrite my life. That thought brings me more power than I have felt in years.

Zoe is strong and loyal. I know she will do the right thing and set the dominoes in motion. I know she will go against my advice and talk to the police. She's always been so independent and righteous. Mummy's little girl. As long as Caitlyn keeps her mouth shut, everything will be alright. But that's the problem with secrets. You can't ever completely control how they will unravel.

Work by Hollie

LoveSick
In the Wake of Night